FROM ONE
EXPERIENCE
TO ANOTHER

FROM ONE EXPERIENCE TO ANOTHER

AWARD-WINNING AUTHORS SHARING REAL-LIFE EXPERIENCES THROUGH FICTION

Edited by

M. Jerry Weiss
& Helen S. Weiss

A Tom Doherty Associates Book / New York

FROM ONE EXPERIENCE TO ANOTHER

This book is printed on acid-free paper.

A Forge Book
Published by Tom Doherty Associates, Inc.
175 Fifth Avenue
New York, NY 10010

Forge® is a registered trademark of Tom Doherty Associates, Inc.

Photo of Sharon Dennis Wyeth on page 161 by Katie McManus, "Teaching K-8"

Design by Lynn Newmark

Library of Congress Cataloging-in-Publication Data

From one experience to another / edited by M. Jerry Weiss & Helen
    S. Weiss.—1st ed.
        p.   cm.
    "A Tom Doherty Associates book."
    Summary: A collection of fifteen short stories in which writers
including Avi, Jay Bennett, Gordon Korman, Joan Lowery Nixon,
and Suzanne Fisher Staples draw upon their own childhood
experiences.
    ISBN 0-312-86253-9 (hardcover : acid-free paper)
    1. Short stories. [1. Short stories.] I. Weiss, M. Jerry
(Morton Jerry), 1926–   . II. Weiss Helen S.
PZ5.F91754 1997
[Fic]—dc21   97-8745
                                                       CIP
                                                        AC

First Edition: September 1997

Printed in the United States of America

0 9 8 7 6 5 4 3 2 1

for Lizzie Gersh and Max Gersh

CONTENTS

Acknowledgments   9
Publisher's Note   11

Jay Bennett   My Brother's Keeper   15
Joan Bauer   The Truth About
                         Sharks   31
Herb Karl   A Game of War   49
Gordon Korman   Hamish Mactavish
                         Is Eating a Bus   57
Walter Dean Myers   Sunrise Over Manaus   73
Joan Lowery Nixon   No Matter What   89
Richard Peck   The Most Important
                         Night of Melanie's
                         Life   105
Susan Beth Pfeffer   Young Blue Eyes   113
Nancy Springer   A Blue Moon in a
                         White Sky   125
Virginia Euwer Wolff   Dozens of Roses:
                         A Story for Voices   141
Suzanne Fisher Staples   Klesmer   147
Sharon Dennis Wyeth   "White" Real Estate   161
Judith Gorog   The Wedding Cake
                         in the Middle of the
                         Road   177
Neal Shusterman   Blue Diamond   187
Avi   Biderbiks Don't Cry   203

About the Authors   221

ACKNOWLEDGMENTS

The gods of writers and readers must have been smiling warmly on the birthing of this book; the project progressed with such ease and good humor from everyone involved. For this we gladly acknowledge and thank two groups: the talented authors who crafted these wonderful stories, cheerfully meeting an almost impossible deadline; the good folks at Forge, with a special nod to Kathleen Doherty and Jonathan Schmidt, for their enthusiasm and efficiency in expediting the process from first phone call to final volume.

For us, this has been a delightful labor, indeed.

Helen S. Weiss
M. Jerry Weiss

But I don't have anything to write about . . .

Every experience in one's life has meaning. Though it is common for most of us to recall most vividly those experiences that prove life-altering, such as marriage or the birth of a child, with age we begin to understand the significance of the smaller, day-to-day events that collectively make us the person we are. But for the young person, who may feel that "nothing ever happens" in his/her life, appreciating the value and significance of common day-to-day experiences is a difficult task to communicate.

From One Experience to Another was created for this reason.

Dr. M. Jerry Weiss, a professor emeritus at Jersey City State College in New Jersey, has for many years taught adolescent literature classes to teachers from around the country. He and Helen Weiss, an author and lecturer, came to me with the idea for this book as a response to a familiar complaint: teachers weren't able to motivate their students to write even the simplest essays about their lives. Why?

"I don't have anything to write about!" It's an all-too-familiar complaint. It seems students are routinely unable to respond to their own lives *imaginatively.*

Jerry and Helen decided that this frustration needed to be addressed—and who better to communicate to young people the value of the everyday in their own lives than fifteen of the most celebrated writers for young people.

It was their hope—and ours—that by reading these stories young people will feel liberated to reconsider their own "non" experiences in a new light—to see that one can find meaning and value in even the smallest or most trivial event. But what it requires is an act of the imagination. And fiction is the surest conduit to the imagination.

Kathleen Doherty
Publisher

FROM ONE
EXPERIENCE
TO ANOTHER

Jay Bennett

A number of years ago, when I was young and played semipro football, I had a teammate who went on to become a star in the pros. We had continued to be close friends all through his career. One night, he called me, in great distress, and asked me to do a favor for him. It meant an awful lot to him and his career. I thought and thought, and then I told him a few days later that I couldn't do it.

This ended our friendship.

Out of this sad experience, I created "My Brother's Keeper." In this story you will see the creative process at work. Instead of being a friend, I became a brother. Well, read and you will see what else I did to take a personal experience and transform it into a new form and being.

My Brother's Keeper

Do you swear to tell the truth and nothing but the truth?"

The truth?

Nothing but the truth?

What is truth?

Jamie raised his hand, his right hand, in the hushed courtroom and as he did that, his senses began to reel, to reel back to the beginning.

The very beginning.

He had been sleeping, a restless sleep and then the clear ring of the telephone cut into him. His eyes slowly opened and he looked about the silent shadowy room, listening to the cold, insistent ring.

He was alone in the dark house.

Completely alone.

His uncle, with whom he lived, had gone off on a fishing trip near the state border.

"If the fishing is fine I'll stay awhile. If it's bad, real bad, I'll come on home. Anyway I'll be back before you go on to college."

Jamie nodded silently.

"I'll drive you up there. See you settled in."

"You don't have to, Harry. I'll manage."

"I know you can. But I want to do it."

Ted's away in his own fantasy world and I'm all you have left, Jamie thought.

"Okay," he said. "You'll take me up there."

The man smiled and started up the motor. Then he waved his lean, tanned hand and was gone.

Jamie was alone.

And now the phone was ringing.

He reached over to the night table and picked up the dark, gleaming receiver.

The summer curtain rustled noiselessly.

Then he heard the voice.

"Jamie?"

A slight chill went through him and he was silent.

"Jamie?"

It was his brother.

His only brother.

"You alone?"

"Yes," Jamie said.

Outside in the distant night a dog began to bark.

A low mournful sound.

Jamie listened to it.

"Uncle Harry?"

"He's gone fishing."

"Where?"

"Upstate. Near the falls."

"Oh."

The barking had stopped and the silence of the long night flooded into the room.

And all the time Jamie waited.

Waited.

For his older brother to tell him.

Then he heard it.

"I'm in trouble, Jamie."

And you need me to bail you out, Jamie thought bitterly.

"Trouble."

This time the voice was almost a whisper.

But Jamie heard it clearly.

His lips thinned into a straight line.

I'm your kid brother. Five long years younger than you are and all the time, all through the years I had to act like I was the older brother.

All the time.

Jamie's hand tightened around the receiver.

"What have you done, Ted?"

"I want to come over and talk."

"You slugged somebody in a bar? A guy came over to get your autograph and he got nasty and you were with a girl and you. . ."

"It's not that," Ted cut in.

"Then what?"

"It . . . it's hard to explain."

Jamie's voice grew harsh.

"Nothing's hard to explain. Tell me now."

"Let me see you. I have to."

Jamie breathed out and looked over at the clock on the night table. The clock Ted had given him as a birthday present along with a thousand-dollar check.

"It's three in the morning," he said. "Let it wait."

"It can't wait."

"What do you mean?"

"I'm coming over. Whether you want me or not. I need you."

There was a slight break in the voice.

And Jamie thought to himself bleakly, this time it must be bad.

Really bad.

"Okay," he said. "Come on over."

"Thanks, Jamie."

Jamie was silent.

"I'll never forget it."

You will, Ted. You will.

You always do.

Then he slowly put the receiver back onto its hook.

He sat there in the dark, narrow room a long time, thinking, ever thinking.

His hand clenched into a tight fist.

Then after a while, the hand unclenched.

And lay hopelessly against Jamie's side.

He let the doorbell ring three times, then he slowly went down the carpeted stairs and walked slowly through the dimly lit corridor to the front door.

His brother stood big and large against the night.

A menacing figure.

But the face was pale and gentle and the eyes haunting.

"Jamie."

And his brother reached out with his large, muscular arms and drew him close.

So very close.

Jamie was tall but his head barely reached Ted's shoulder.

He felt a deep tremor of love for the big man and then the tremor was gone.

The bleak feeling was back within him.

"I need you. Need you a lot," Ted murmured.

Jamie slowly drew away.

"Let's go into the kitchen and have a cup of coffee, Ted. You look like you could use one."

"Sure. Whatever you say."

"Then we'll talk," Jamie said softly.

"Anything. Anything you say."

Then Ted followed his smaller brother into the neat, yellow kitchen, lifted a heavy wooden chair, swung it about, set it down without a sound and slid into it gracefully.

It was all done in one smooth, flowing motion.

And watching him, Jamie thought of the times he had watched Ted weave and run and evade tacklers with an effortless grace.

The crowd in the packed stands roaring.

His teammates on the sidelines jumping with their hands raised high against a cold autumn sky.

And Jamie thought how on the football field Ted loomed large, so very large.

In full control of himself.

So very well put together.

So finely disciplined.

Rarely making a wrong move.

Every inch a rounded, mature man.

But once he stepped off the field and took off his uniform, he became a child.

A huge, gentle child.

Who got himself into scrapes and had to be bailed out.

Again and again.

Jamie lighted the jet under the coffeepot.

"What's it this time?"

Ted looked at his brother's trim, straight back and didn't speak.

Jamie was tall and slender, his fine-featured face with the ever-somber look on it always made him appear older than his eighteen years.

Ted fondly called him "Straight Arrow."

"Tell me, Ted."

"I . . . I hit a man."

Jamie stared at the blue jet on the gas range.

His voice was low when he spoke.

"Another bar fight? You're not a drinker. How do you get into these things?"

"No, Jamie," Ted murmured.

"Then what?"

"I was driving on Desmond Street and I . . . I hit a man."

Jamie didn't turn.

"He was drunk and he walked in front of the car. It was very dark and nobody was around. You know how deserted Desmond Street is. You know, Jamie. You know. Dark and deserted and . . . and. . . ."

His voice tailed off into the silence.

Jamie's hands gripped the top of the white range.

The range was hot to the touch but he didn't feel it.

Then he heard his brother speak again.

"I was sober. Clean sober. It's the truth, Jamie. The truth."

"And?"

"I panicked and left him lying there."

Jamie swung about sharply.

His face white and tense.

His voice cold and harsh.

"What in the hell are you saying? What?"

The tears came into Ted's eyes.

His gentle blue eyes.

"I . . . I panicked."

Jamie came swiftly over to him.

"And you left him there?" he shouted.

His angry voice filled the narrow room.

Ted shivered.

His lips trembled.

"How? How could you do that?"

The big man looked up to him pleadingly.

When he spoke, his voice was low, very low.

As if he was talking to himself.

"I . . . I lost my head. . . . It wasn't my fault. He walked in front of the car. He was drunk. Drunk. Came out of the night. From nowhere. I wasn't going fast. I wasn't. I swear to you on Dad and Mom's graves that I. . ."

Jamie fiercely cut into him.

"You left him lying in the street? In the street?"

"There was nobody around. Nobody saw it. That's all that was in my mind."

"And you drove off?"

"All I was thinking of was my career and nobody saw it. I wasn't myself. You know I'm not like that. You know it. I help everybody. Everybody. I haven't a mean feeling in my . . . I wasn't myself."

He hit his knee with his big hand again and again.

"I got scared. Scared. I wasn't myself. I wasn't."

Jamie reached down and fiercely grabbed him by his shirt.

"But he was a human being. Not a dog. You don't even leave a dog lying in the street and run off."

"It all happened so fast. I couldn't handle it. Just couldn't."

Jamie slowly let go of the shirt and drew back.

"Was he dead?"

And he felt inside of him the heavy beating of his heart while he waited for the answer.

And also mixed within was an overwhelming pity for his lost brother.

Then he heard the words.

"No. Just hurt."

Jamie breathed out silently.

"Badly hurt?"

Ted shook his head and then ran his hand through his curly blond hair before answering.

"Just hurt."

"How do you know that?"

"I went back. Walked. And there was an ambulance there. I stood where nobody could see me."

"And?"

"I could make out what was happening."

"He was hurt enough to be taken to a hospital," Jamie said sharply.

"He was."

Jamie's voice rose.

"In Christ's name, why didn't you come out of the dark and go over there and face it?"

"I . . . I just couldn't."

"The truth. All you needed was to tell them the truth. The truth."

"Couldn't do it. Just. . ."

And Jamie, looking at him, knew that he couldn't.

You're lost, Ted.

Lost.

Ever since Mom and Dad were killed in that crash.

You never got over it.

And you turned to me.

To me.

When Jamie spoke again, his voice was gentle.

"And then what did you do?"

"I went back to the car and drove away. Nobody saw me."

Jamie went over to the window and stared out into the night.

The dark, cloudless night.

He did it this time, Jamie thought.

He really did it.

Jamie heard his brother's voice drift over to him.

"I spoke to Carmody."

"Who is he?"

"The team's lawyer. He wants to talk to you."

"To me? Why?"

"He . . . he said he'd explain to you."

"Explain what to me?"

Ted looked at him and didn't answer.

"Tell me."

"I don't know. I really don't know."

"You do."

"I swear to you on Mom's. . ."

Jamie cut in savagely.

"Don't swear. Leave Mom and Dad out of this. Let them sleep in peace. Thank God, they're long dead. Dead and away from you."

"Jamie, please don't talk to me that way. Please don't do it."

"You make me."

He came over to the table and sat down heavily and then looked across it at the big man.

"I'm tired of you, Ted," he said.

"Please, Jamie. Don't say that."

And the desperate lost look in his brother's eyes pierced through him.

"Jamie, don't leave me alone."

Jamie looked away from him and out to the night.

"I can't make it without you."

I know.

How well I know it.

"When does this Carmody want me to talk to him?"

"In the morning. Anytime you choose."

"Okay," Jamie murmured desolately. "I'll see him."

"Thanks."

That's all the big man said.

And Jamie knew that he was too full of emotion to say any-more.

"Get upstairs," Jamie suddenly shouted.

Ted looked fearfully at him and didn't speak.

"Get to bed and try to get some rest. You look like a damned wreck."

Ted slowly rose.

"Sure, Jamie. Sure."

Then Jamie watched him turn and go to the stairs.

Watched him as he swung on the second step, swung around, with that smooth, graceful motion, and then stood stock-still and stared bewilderedly about him as if he didn't know where he was.

"I'm sorry, Jamie," he said. "I always bring you trouble. I'm sorry."

Then Jamie watched him go up the steps and out of sight.

Jamie was now alone in the night-filled room.

Thinking.

Ever thinking.

The truth.

Nothing but the truth.

*   *   *

"Ted claims that nobody saw him. Nobody."

"That's right," Ted murmured.

The lawyer turned to him.

"But soon somebody will come forward and say that he or she did see you in the car. It's happened before in my practice. And I've been a lawyer a long, long time."

Jamie sat waiting.

Carmody spoke again.

"We must be ready."

Ready for what? Jamie thought bleakly.

They were sitting in the high-ceilinged, elaborately furnished office.

The three of them.

Carmody, Ted, and Jamie.

The door of the room was closed.

Tightly closed.

Carmody was a lithe, tanned man with dark alert eyes and a quiet, self-assured voice.

"So far the police have no clues. Not a one."

It's early, Jamie thought somberly.

"I have some good friends there who will tell me if they come up with any. Such as a license-plate number."

Carmody lit a cigarette and paused.

Then he turned to Jamie.

And quietly studied him.

He spoke.

"I understand that you were valedictorian in your graduating class."

"I was," Jamie said.

"And you've been accepted to a very prestigious college."

"Yale."

"He's getting a full scholarship. I told you that," Ted said proudly.

Carmody smiled.

"You did, Ted."

He puffed at his cigarette.

"There's not a blemish on your record, Jamie."

He pronounced the word "blemish" softly.

So very softly.

And Jamie knew instantly that he disliked the man.

Disliked him intensely.

Carmody spoke again.

"Your brother needs your help. Needs it badly."

"What does he need?"

"For you to say that he was with you on the night of the accident."

Jamie stared silently at the man.

The room had grown still.

Very still.

Ted had risen from his chair, a wild, anguished look on his face.

Carmody's voice cut through the stillness.

"Ted was with you all night long. Every minute of it. Never leaving you."

Ted walked over to the lawyer.

"You didn't tell me that Jamie would have to do that."

"We've no choice."

Ted loomed over the man.

"But it's against all he stands for. I know him. I don't want it."

Carmody snuffed out his cigarette, slowly and deliberately.

"You'll do as I tell you."

"No. I won't hold still for this."

"You'll have to."

Ted pounded the desk with his big fist.

"No. No."

His face was pale and sweat glistened on his forehead.

"Keep quiet and sit down."

Ted's big hands began to tremble.

"Sit," Carmody commanded.

The big man slowly turned and went back to his seat.

Carmody's voice when he spoke was precise and clean.

His eyes cold and impassive.

"Listen to me. There's a real world out there. So listen. The two of you."

He paused and then went on.

"Ted, you are one of the young stars of pro football today. You made three million dollars your first year. You will make much, much more as you play on. You are sure to become the club's most valuable property."

The real world, Jamie thought bitterly.

The real world has its own truth.

But, dammit, I have my own.

My own.

Carmody was speaking.

". . . Ted, you did a damn fool thing. I believe you. It was not your fault. You panicked. But you drove away and left a man lying on the street, not knowing whether he was dead or alive."

"Lost my head. Lost it," Ted murmured.

"I know and understand. But you're going to be called into court. And when that happens I want to be there at your side with an airtight alibi. And no matter what they come up with, that alibi will pull us through. Do you hear me?"

Ted bowed his head and covered his face with his hands.

"I'll pull you through. I will."

Carmody turned to Jamie.

"You say you care for your brother."

"Yes."

"Then you must do this."

"Must?"

"Yes. I assure you that nothing will happen to you or him. Nothing."

"You know from experience?"

Carmody nodded.

"I know. Well, Jamie?"

Jamie looked away to Ted and didn't answer.

He heard Carmody's voice.

"If you're thinking of the man who was injured . . . ?"

"I am."

Carmody smiled.

"He's going to fully recover. And then he's going to be quietly well taken care of. It will turn out to be the best thing that has ever happened to him."

He leaned forward to Jamie.

"Well?"

"Let's wait and see what happens," Jamie said.

"But we can count on you?"

Jamie looked from Carmody over to his brother.

Ted still sat there, his head bowed, his face still covered by his big hands.

Jamie turned back to the lawyer.

"You can count on me."

"After the crash, when I came to get the two of you and take you home with me. . ."

Uncle Harry paused and looked out over the lake and didn't speak for a while.

His lean, lined face was tight and sad.

Jamie waited for him to speak again.

"It just tore my heart out. I reached over to get his hand but he turned away from me and went to you. And he stood there looking down into your face and then he reached out to you and held you and cried. And all the while you stood there, holding him, your face tight and silent. Like you were a big man, sheltering him."

The sun was still high and the lake rippled, ripples of gold.

Uncle Harry cast his line out again.

"He needs you. He'll always need you."

Then he said, "I can't tell you what to do, Jamie. It's your call."

"And you think it will work out like the lawyer says?"

Harry nodded.

"You'll end up in court in the witness chair. That's if you decide to go along with them."

"You can't help me decide?"

He shook his head.

"I'd give my right arm to help you decide. But I just can't. It's your call, Jamie. Yours alone."

He got up.

"I don't feel like fishing anymore. Let's pack up and go home."

He reeled in his line.

"It's getting cloudy anyway."

But the sun was shining.

Very brightly.

The voice pierced the dead silence of the courtroom.

"Do you swear to tell the truth and nothing but the truth?"

Jamie raised his right hand and looked over to where Ted sat.

The haunted, pleading look in Ted's eyes.

He knew that he would remember that look for the rest of his life.

But within he said:

I can't do it, Ted.

I just can't.

And Jamie knew that he could never again be his brother's keeper.

The tears came to his eyes.

And he bowed his head.

Joan Bauer

It happened when I was nineteen years old. For some reason it has stayed with me through the years. I have tried to work it out in my mind, tried to rescript the event, but the anger of the thing remains with me and I remember it every time I see a sign in a store that reads SHOPLIFTERS WILL BE PROSECUTED TO THE FULL EXTENT OF THE LAW.

I was falsely accused of shoplifting.

I remember it still so clearly. I was at a big department store in Oak Park, Illinois, a store where I had shopped often, where my mother and grandmother had shopped as girls, a store that had good memories for me and my family. It was autumn and I was in a hurry to buy a pair of pants. I tried on a pair that I liked, told the saleswoman I was going to buy them, headed toward a rack of clothing near the elevator still wearing the pants, and was dragged down to a basement security room by a female security guard who said I was a thief and kept repeating, "That's not the way we play the game." I handled none of it well. My mind went blank. She ordered me to take the slacks off and I did, humiliated, sitting in a scratched folding chair in my underpants while she smirked at me. Someone finally brought my own slacks to me and I was let go with a warning to never set foot in the store again. When I returned to the store with my mother to complain to the manager, we were given a partial apology, despite the fact that the saleswoman who'd been waiting on me said there had been a mistake. Then, to cap it off, a relative made it clear she never believed my innocence.

I offer here a fictional rescripting of this tale. The beauty of fiction is that it can allow the writer to have power over past experiences. I wish I had responded the way my fictional character Beth does, but the fact that I wrote her lines and gave her courage is gift enough for me.

The Truth About Sharks

The noise seemed faraway at first, like a foghorn blaring in the distance. It was a persistent, ringing, irritating sound. I hated it. I pulled my down comforter over my head, but the noise got louder. It would continue to get louder, too, until I did something. I lifted my head from beneath the covers and saw unhappily that it was morning. I did not do morning, being a devout night person. I gripped the sides of the bed to steady my angst-ridden body and lumbered toward my closet as the noise got louder.

"I hate this!"

I threw open the closet door, lamely stretched my arms upward to find the source of the noise and turn it off, but my mother, the rat, had hidden it well this time. I searched through shoe boxes, purses, then I found it. I grabbed the alarm clock and pushed the on button to off.

Silence.

I dropped to the floor ignoring the knock on my door. All noises were unwelcome in the morning. My smiling mother opened the door and regarded me slumped on the floor.

"There you are."

I shook my head. "It's a mirage."

"Beth," said my mother, "the day has begun; I suggest you do the same. You have to go shopping, wash the dog. . . ."

My mother is a morning person. I made a pitiful noise and curled into a ball.

"Don't push my buttons, Beth. The party starts at five."

I sighed deeply, indicating my level of stress. I didn't see why I had to go to Uncle Al's birthday party that would be nothing but torture because Uncle Al was, basically, subterranean.

"And," my mother ordered, "don't say anything about this party either because Al is my brother who has his faults like all of us do. . . ."

I don't tell sexist jokes at the dinner table.

I don't suck food through my teeth.

"And we're going to go and honor him and make it very clear that we love him."

Nothing came from my lips.

Mother stared at my lips just to make sure nothing would. "You can have the car, Beth, from now until one, then I absolutely have to have it."

"It's ten-thirty already."

"Then you'd better get cracking."

"I hate mornings."

"What a joy you are to me," Mom said and walked off.

I pulled my best black pants from their hanger, the pants I had spent a fortune on, the black pants that now hung dull and lifeless, hopelessly stained by guacamole dip that was dumped on me and them in sheer hostility by Edgar Bromfman when he was doing his Ostrich in Search of a Mate imitation at Darla Larchmont's party. I loved those slacks. They had power.

Once.

They went with my best beaded vest that I wanted to wear to Uncle Al's party because Bianca, my hideous cousin who always dressed to kill, would be there with her latest gorgeous boyfriend to snub me and make me feel insignificant and toady. She learned this from Uncle Al, her father.

Reingold, my black toy poodle, whined torturously at the door. I let him crash in, a rollicking, teeny ball of fur. I picked him up.

"Reingold, you who see all and know all, tell me where in Fairfield County, Connecticut, I can get a vastly important pair of black power pants."

Reingold licked my neck and wiggled.

"Reingold, your wisdom exceeds even your cuteness. Of course, I will go to that new store on Route 1 in Norwalk. And there I will find them."

Reingold followed me into the bathroom. I gave him a drink of water from a little Dixie cup, washed my face fast, brushed my oily brown hair that hung exhausted on my shoulders; I threw on gray sweats. There was no doubt about it, I looked seedy.

"You're going out like that?" Mom asked, staring.

"Yes." Beauty would come later. All I had going for me now was personality.

Mom touched my bangs. "Maybe if you just—"

I put on sunglasses. "I won't see anyone we know."

Mitchell Gail's was a huge store; five stories, to be exact, with too many choices. My mother said that was the problem with the world today—too many choices. Paper or plastic? Regular, premium, or super? Small, medium, or grande?

I walked past the stocky, stern security guard who was picking her teeth, a visual reminder of Uncle Al's bash tonight. Maybe they knew each other. She glared at me through frigid, gray eyes and touched her name tag, MADGE P. GROTON, SECURITY GUARD. The woman needed a life. The sign above her read, SHOPLIFTERS WILL BE PROSECUTED TO THE FULL EXTENT OF THE LAW. I should hope so. I caught sight of myself in a full-length mirror. Who would know that beneath the greasy hair, sallow skin, and baggy sweats there lived a person of depth and significance? I groaned at my vile reflection and headed for the pants section.

I found four pairs of black slacks, size 10, and one pair, size 8. Hope springs eternal. I walked into the dressing room, past another larger, more threatening sign—SHOPLIFTERS WILL BE PROSECUTED TO THE FULL EXTENT OF THE LAW—just in case any thieves missed the first warning. A sweet, round saleswoman showed me to an empty changing room. Her name tag read HANNAH. She had sad eyes.

"If you need anything I'll help you," Hannah said.

"Thanks."

She looked down.

"Must be the pits working on Saturday," I offered.

She shook her head. "I'd rather work. It's better than sitting home. My boyfriend was cheating on me with this manicurist. I saw them kissing in his apartment."

"I'm sorry."

She laughed, not happily. "He said he never really loved me; I was too fat." She looked at her plump arms.

"He's a jerk. You're not fat."

"I'm just going to work, save my money—"

"—Hannah!" It was the store manager. Hannah shrugged stiffly, let out a long, painful breath, and left.

Males. I was between them at the moment. Probably just as well given my last boyfriend's sizzling attraction to blondes—a little problem we were never able to work out since I'm a brunette. I observed a moment of silence for Hannah's pain. Then I tried on the size 8 pants. I could zip them up exactly one-eighth of an inch.

Okay . . . size 8 is still a dream.

On went a size 10.

No.

Another. . . .

Thunder-thighs.

The fourth pair hit me mid-calf.

I tried the fifth. Not bad. I turned in front of the mirror. Not perfect, but doable. And with my beaded vest these could be downright smashing. I put on my shoes, left my coat and sweatpants in the changing room with my purse underneath them. I shouldn't leave my purse there, but I was in such a hurry. I said to Hannah, "I'll take these, but I'm going to keep looking."

"They look nice on you."

They do, don't they? I smiled at the beckoning sale sign over a rack of pants right by the elevator that I'd not seen before. I walked toward the rack and was just reaching for an excellent pair of size 10 black silk pants marked 50 percent off, which would keep me within my budget, which would be a miracle, when a rough hand came down hard on my shoulder and spun me around.

"That's not the way we play the game," Madge P. Groton, Security Guard, barked.

"What?"

"That's not the way we play the game," she repeated, pulling my hands behind my back and pushing me forward.

"What are you talking about?"

She was strong. She pushed me past a line of staring customers, into the elevator. She squeezed my hands hard. A cold fear swept through me.

"What," I shouted, *"are you doing?"*

"You were going into the elevator wearing pants you didn't pay for. We call that shoplifting around here."

"No, I was—"

She pressed my hands tighter.

"You're hurting me!"

"Shut up!"

Tears stung my eyes. My chest was pounding. I had seen a TV show about what to do if you're falsely arrested. You don't fight, you calmly explain your position. There was an explanation. I would give the explanation to this person at the right time and I would go home and never set foot in this store again. If I panicked now. . .

The elevator door opened and the guard shoved me forward past the jewelry counter like a mass murderer, past Mrs. Applegate, Uncle Al's nosy neighbor, who stared at me like she wasn't surprised.

"Ma'am, I'm *innocent,*" I said.

"Yeah, and I'm the Easter Bunny." She opened a door that read SECURITY, and pushed me inside to a dingy beige windowless room with the now-familiar sign: SHOPLIFTERS WILL BE PROSECUTED TO THE FULL EXTENT OF THE LAW.

"Please, Ma'am, Ms. Groton . . ."

My whole body was shaking.

"Take them off," she snarled.

"What?"

"Take the pants off. Now."

I stared at her. "You mean here?"

She put her hand on her gun. This was crazy.

"I get a phone call, right?"

"You are in possession of stolen property."

"Ma'am, I know you're trying to do your job. Just listen to me. I was going to buy these pants. I told this to the saleswoman. I left my coat and my pants and my purse in the changing room. Believe me, this is a big—"

"Take them off." She leaned back in her chair, enjoying her power.

I felt my face shaking like tears were exploding inside. I was sick and terrified. My mind reached for anything.

I remembered that article I'd read about sharks. If you're swimming in the ocean and a shark comes at you to attack, hit him in the nose, the expert said.

I looked at Madge P. Groton, Security Shark.

"No, Ma'am. Not until I get my pants back."

She leaned toward me; her face was tight and mean. "You do what I tell you."

I took a huge breath and looked at her hard.

"No, Ma'am."

Her face darkened. She punched a button on a large black phone, said into the receiver, "I've got one. Send a car."

Nausea hit. I choked down vomit. My heart was beating out of my chest. Madge P. Groton, Security Guard, took her handcuffs off her belt and clinked them on the cracked linoleum floor again and again.

"If we could just talk to that saleswoman," I tried, "I think we could clear this—"

"That's not the way we play the game."

I leaned against the wall and pushed down the screaming voice inside that shouted I was innocent because Madge P. Groton had made up her mind and the Easter Bunny himself couldn't change it. And a car was coming for me with police, probably, which meant jail, probably. I could get thrown into jail with dangerous people and no one was going to listen. I'd never get into veterinary school, never see my dreams fulfilled. My life was over at seventeen.

"I need to make a phone call, Ma'am. I need to call my mother."

"I bet you would."

"The law says I get to make a phone call."

"You can do it at the station."

"Ma'am, my purse and coat and pants are still in the changing room."

Nothing.

I checked my watch: 1:10. My mother was waiting for the car. She wouldn't be getting it soon. I lowered my head and started to cry.

"I've seen you kids," she snarled. "You think you can take

anything you want, call your parents, cry some fake tears, and it's over, huh? You think wrong."

"I didn't do it."

I jumped at the harsh knock on the door. A big policeman with leathery skin entered with his hand on his gun. He listened to the security guard's story. I told him she'd made a mistake, but it didn't seem to matter. No one believes prisoners.

"Don't ever set foot in this store again," warned Madge P. Groton.

Don't worry, lady.

The policeman took my arm firmly and we walked out of the store, past Mrs. Applegate, past jewelry, and purses, and leather gloves, and scarves, past the Clinique counter with those white-jacketed technicians, to the waiting police car.

"You have the right to remain silent," he said the sickening words to me. "You have the right to an attorney. If you do not have an attorney, one will be appointed for you."

He opened the back door of the squad car, I got in crying.

The door shut like a prison gate.

"It wasn't worth it, Miss," he said, got into the front and drove off with Mrs. Applegate staring after us.

I slumped down deep in the seat and looked at my feet because I was sure everyone I'd ever met in my entire, complex life saw me in the prisoner section of the squad car.

"Officer," I whispered, "I know you're doing your job. I know that security guard was doing hers, but I've got to tell you, if we go back to that store, I've got a witness who knows that I didn't do it."

This was a definite gamble. I didn't know if that saleswoman would remember me.

"Who?" he asked.

I told him about the saleswoman. "Officer, I am really scared and I don't know what else to do. Would you let me try to prove I'm innocent?"

He stopped the car and stared at me through the grill.

"Look, sir, I know I look really weird. I had to buy some slacks for my uncle's stupid birthday party and my mother needed the car in a hurry, so I just jumped out of bed and hadn't figured on getting arrested. I mean, I normally bathe. I normally look better than this. Corpses look better than I do right now. I sound like an idiot."

The policeman searched my face. "Which salesperson?"

I put my two innocent hands on the grill. "Her name was Helen. No. Hortense. Wait—*Hannah*. Yes! She had just broken up with her boyfriend who had been cheating on her for months with this manicurist and he said he'd never really loved her because she was too fat, which she wasn't—a little plump, maybe, but definitely not fat—and she was giving up men. At least for the moment."

He stared at me.

"Not that men are bad. I mean, some are. But you know that. You arrest bad people and that's a really good thing."

I was digging my own grave. He would take me to the psychiatric hospital. I would be locked in a room with no sharp objects. I looked away.

"*Please* believe me, Officer. I'm not really this strange!"

The officer sighed deeply. "I don't have time for this." He rammed the patrol car into gear, did a perfect U-turn, and headed back toward Mitchell Gail's.

"Oh, thank you, Officer! You are a wonderful person, a—"

He held up his hand for me to stop. I bit my tongue. I didn't ask what would happen if Hannah wasn't there or didn't remember me or was Madge P. Groton's best friend.

"Don't try anything funny," said the officer as he opened the squad car prisoner door and I got out.

"I won't." This was the most humorless situation I'd ever been in.

"I do the talking."

I nodded wildly. We walked through the front door, past jewelry, purses, and Madge P. Groton, who nearly dropped her fangs when she saw us.

"Just checking something out," said the officer to her and kept on walking to the elevator.

"What floor were you on?" he asked me.

I held up four trembling fingers.

"You can talk when I talk to you."

"Right," I croaked.

The elevator came and Madge P. Groton glared at us with poison death darts as we got in. I figured an actual policeman was more powerful in the food chain than a security guard, but I decided not to ask at this moment.

The elevator stopped at every floor. A little girl got on with her mother, looked at me and said, "What's the matter with her, Mommy?"

"Polly," said the mother, "don't be rude."

The elevator opened at the fourth floor. We got out. My eyes searched for Hannah. The policeman walked up to a gray-haired saleswoman.

"We're looking for Hortense," he said.

"*Hannah!*" I shrieked.

The woman pointed to Hannah who was folding sweaters and arranging them on a shelf. We walked toward her. Remember me? I wanted to shout. I am the person who took time from my busy schedule to listen to your problems with your scuzzy boyfriend; the person who cared enough to show you the healing touch of humanity during a particularly stress-packed morning in my life.

"Do you know this young woman?" the policeman asked Hannah.

Hannah looked at me and smiled. "I waited on her this morning. She left her purse and coat and stuff in the changing room. I've got them for you."

Marge P. Groton stormed up. "What's going on?"

"Just clearing a few things up," said the officer.

Madge P. Groton dug in her spurs. "This girl is a shoplifter. I caught her trying to leave the store wearing merchandise!"

Hannah looked shocked. "Then why would she leave her purse in the changing room?"

Why indeed?

I smiled broadly at Madge P. Groton, Security Guard, whose face had turned a delightful funeral gray.

"And why would she leave her coat?" Hannah continued. "It's worth at least as much as the pants. You made a mistake, Madge."

"Can I see the purse?" asked the officer.

Hannah ran to get it. I winced as he pulled out Tums, dental floss, breath mints, two hairbrushes, my giant panda key ring, a box of Milk Duds, three packs of tissues, my sunglasses, four lipsticks.

"You got a wallet in here?"

I reached deep within and pulled it out. He checked my driver's license. He counted the money. Seventy-five dollars.

"I think," said the officer, "we've got things straightened out here, wouldn't you say so, Ms. Groton?"

Madge P. Groton sputtered first. Her wide jaw locked. Her thick neck gripped. Her nose mole twitched. She turned on her scuffed heel and stormed off. The officer gave me back my purse, coat. "You're free to go," he said. "Just give the store back the pants."

"I never want to see these pants again. Thank you for believing me, Officer . . . um . . . I don't know your name."

"Brennerman."

What a wonderful name. I thanked him again.

I thanked Hannah.

I thanked God.

I ran into the changing room, put on my dear, old gray grubbies, drew a penetrating breath of freedom, and raced toward my mother's Taurus. It was two-thirty. All I had to worry about now was the flaming war spear my mother would have singeing the lawn in honor of my late return.

I floored the Taurus, most unwise, since I'd had one brush with the law already today. I drove home, three miles under the speed limit (a first), thanking God I was a free American.

I turned left at the Dunkin' Donuts on Route 1 feeling something wasn't quite right.

I stared at the poster of the cholesterol-laden Dunkin' Munchkins nestled cozily in their box as the unrighteousness of it grew in my soul.

I'd been publicly humiliated.

Falsely accused.

I have my rights!

I rammed Mom's car around and headed back for Mitchell Gail's.

I am teenager, hear me roar.

I parked the car, stormed into the store past the SHOPLIFTERS WILL BE PROSECUTED TO THE FULL EXTENT OF THE LAW sign, right past Madge P. Groton, Security Neanderthal, to the Clinique counter.

"I need to see the store manager," I announced to a blond woman demonstrating face cream. "Immediately."

"Third floor, left by Donna Karan, left by lingerie, you're there."

Madge P. Groton was now guarding the elevator. I took the stairs two at a time, rounded left by Donna Karan, left by lingerie to the store office.

"Can I help you?" asked a tired receptionist with too red hair.

"Only if you're in charge, Ma'am. I need to see the manager."

She looked me up and down. "He's busy now." She looked toward the manager's closed office door. The sign read: THOMAS LUNDGREN, STORE MANAGER.

"It can't wait."

"I'm afraid it's going to have to, dear, you see . . ."

"No, Ma'am. You see. I was falsely arrested in this store by Madge P. Groton, Security Witch, and in exactly two seconds I'm going to call a very large lawyer."

"Oh, Mr. Lundgren!" the woman's bony hands fluttered in front of her face. She flew into his office. I walked in behind her. "We have a little problem."

Thomas Lundgren, Store Manager, appraised my grubby gray sweats, unimpressed. "What problem is that?" he said coarsely, not getting up.

I told him. The policeman, Hannah, Madge, the lawyer.

He got up.

"Sit down," he purred at me. "Make yourself comfortable. Would you like a soda? *Candy?*"

"I'd like an apology."

"Well, of course, we at Mitchell Gail's are appalled at anything that could be misconstrued—"

"—This wasn't misconstrued."

"We'll have to check this out, of course."

I folded my arms. "I'll wait, Mr. Lundgren."

"Call me Tom." He snapped his finger at the receptionist. "Get Madge up here."

I crossed my legs. "I'd call the police, too, Tom. Officer Brennerman. He's probably the most important one, next to the lawyer."

Tom grew pale; the receptionist twittered. "Make this happen, Celia," he barked. Then he smiled at me big and wide.

"We certainly pride ourselves on treating our customers well."

I smiled back and didn't say he had a long way to go in that department. The phone buzzed and Tom lunged for it. Maybe I'd can veterinary school and become a lawyer. Lawyers have power. No one gets worked up when you say you're going to call a veterinarian.

"I see." Tom said into the receiver. "I see. . . . Yes, Officer Brennerman, it was most unfortunate . . . a vast misunderstanding . . . thank you." He pushed a stick of Wrigley's toward me and mouthed, "Gum?"

I shook my head. Madge P. Groton had seeped into the hall. I said, "By the way, Tom, in addition to false accusations and public humiliation, your security guard told me to take off my pants in her office."

"Pardon?"

"It was a low moment, Tom."

"Tell me you kept them on."

I nodded as Tom moved shakily to the hall, his arms outstretched. "Madge, what is this I'm hearing?"

He shut the office door.

There were hushed, snarling words that I couldn't make out.

I racked my brain to think if I knew any lawyers, large or otherwise. I sort of knew Mr. Heywood down the street, but he was a tax lawyer.

The door opened. Tom grinned. "Madge is truly sorry for the misunderstanding."

Madge glowered at me from the hall. She didn't look sorry.

"Mitchell Gail's is terribly sorry for the . . . inconvenience," he murmured.

"Um, it was a bit more than an inconvenience."

"We would like you to accept a $250 gift certificate from the store for your trouble."

I thought about that.

"We'd be happy to make it $500 for all your trouble," Tom added quickly.

"I'll think about it, Tom."

"We'd really like to get this worked out here and now."

"I'm sure you would, Tom, but I'm going to think about it."

I walked into the hall, past Madge P. Groton, who was so penitent she looked like she'd bitten into a rancid lemon; past Celia, who was fluttering by the receptionist desk. I walked down the stairs and out the door.

Yes!

It was three thirty-seven. All I had to fear now was my mother. I rehearsed my poignant speech all the way home. I was encouraged pulling into the driveway that there was no flaming spear on the lawn. Only a mother spitting fire.

"Mother, you're never going to believe what happened to—"

"You're dead."

I wasn't, of course. Even a profoundly angry parent cannot stay that way long when their beloved child has been falsely accused. It was all I could do to prevent Mom from driving back to the store and personally annihilating Madge P. Groton.

I was the hit of Uncle Al's party. I wore an old black dress, but there was something shining in my face that I could feel— something, Mom said, that money could not buy—empowerment. Mrs. Applegate had called my Aunt Cassie to report on my shoplifting, and even though Aunt Cassie had questioned my innocence, when I told her about Officer Brennerman, she turned pink and flustered and hurried away. I even took Uncle Al aside and told him that the joke he told before dinner offended me and all women through the ages and he *apologized*.

As for my cousin Bianca, she will probably always have a

more glamorous life than me, but for a few brief moments that night it really didn't matter.

And regarding Tom and Madge, I decided to not call a lawyer. Tom upped the gift certificate to $650 and had Madge P. Groton personally apologize to me, which was like watching a vulture telling a half-eaten mouse that he didn't really mean it.

"I'm sorry for the trouble," she snarled.

Tom glared at her.

"It was wrong of me," she added flatly.

"Thank you," I said.

Madge P. Groton backed out the door fast and ran down the hall. It was a great moment. Tom said she was going to work in another store and hoped that I would come in often and bring all my friends. I hoped the store was in Antarctica.

I clutched my $650 gift certificate and embraced budget-free shopping. I found the black pants that had started all the trouble—they were marked down 40 percent now—so I got them along with a cherry-apple-red pants suit and a leather jacket and four pairs of shoes and a silk blouse for my mother, who kept saying how proud she was that I had handled this by myself.

I guess I'd learned the truth about sharks: If one comes barreling at you, the best thing to do is hit it in the nose.

Herb Karl

Part of my youth was spent near the coast of Southeast Florida. I came to live there when my parents migrated from a small town just north of New York City. It took a while, but I learned to appreciate the strange topography and the exotic plants and wildlife. As a newcomer, though, I was sometimes the victim of practical jokes (they'd be called "sick" jokes today)—one of which was the catalyst for "A Game of War."

Two young friends who were lifelong natives of the area lured me into a situation not unlike that experienced by Wilson in the story. It seems that bog pits are one of the natural wonders of South Florida. They look particularly harmless after a dry spell—"resembling a thin layer of mud after the sun has baked out the moisture."

While the image of me thrashing around in the black ooze, fearing for my life, is certainly something I'll never forget, the event alone was not enough for a story. I had to create a complete story line (with a beginning, middle, and end), as well as characters who were capable of generating conflict within themselves and between each other. So I came up with a plot that guaranteed the gamut of emotions displayed by the characters in the story—envy, pride, arrogance, deceit, fear, anger, retribution, rebirth, and friendship. The plot: Three boys playing "war" on a hot summer afternoon become embroiled in an argument over who won. Eventually, they resume the battle on "foreign" soil. Who ultimately wins and what it means to win are left for the reader to decide.

An historical note: The story was conceived at a time when the toys of war were still plentiful and the game of war was popular among pre-adolescent boys. It was also a time when a very real and very unpopular war was being fought by grown men.

In some ways, things haven't changed all that much. Real wars continue to be fought, and we still find them a sad and dreadfully futile way of settling arguments.

The games of war also continue—though the games of the past (which required a lot of real estate) have been supplanted by the electronic combat of Nintendo and Sega Genesis. Incidentally, if someone doesn't write a story pretty soon about the more recent phenomena of paintball and super soakers, I may have to do it myself.

A Game of War

"You're dead, Wilson."

"You missed me."

"I seen you stick your head up, Wilson."

"You missed me."

"Come on, Wilson—you know you're dead. Ask Matt."

"Yeah, Wilson, you're dead. Cope got you when you stuck your head up."

"I told you so."

"I ain't dead."

The three boys stood facing each other on the white sand flat. They carried plastic weapons, barrels pointing down. Overhead, the tropical sun burned furiously in a cloudless sky. They could feel the heat from the sand cooking the soles of their sneakers.

Matt, the oldest of the three, lifted the bottom of his T-shirt and mopped his face. He brought the edge of the shirt to his mouth and sucked from it the briny taste of his own sweat. "I'm going home," he said. "It's too hot."

Cope, the runt of the three, had also had enough. "I got to have some water. I can't hardly talk." He bent over to remove a cluster of burrs which had gathered near the cuff of his trousers. The ones on his sneakers he left alone. They had a way of entwining themselves with the laces.

Wilson wasn't ready to give in—to the sun or to his companions. "You guys ain't quitting just 'cause I won the battle?"

"It's too hot," Matt said. He knelt and placed the palm of his hand on the sand as though to make sure the heat was no illusion.

Wilson cursed under his breath. He was younger than Matt, but physically he was the older boy's equal. Wilson, though, was not the leader. Matt was the leader.

"Besides, you're dead, Wilson," Cope said. "I got you when you stuck your head up."

Wilson fixed his eyes on Cope. "I say you're a liar," he said, brushing back a tuft of wet hair that had fallen across his forehead.

Cope glanced at Matt, then turned to Wilson. "Who you calling a liar?"

"Let's go," Matt interrupted. "It's too hot." He was already on the move, his pace slowed by the sand which clutched at his shoes. The other two followed but not before their eyes spoke of feelings neither fully understood.

The sand flat eventually gave way to a steep dune. The boys climbed to the top where the dune fell off abruptly, forming a gully. With Matt leading, they descended into the gully, then scaled the opposite slope and came out on the shoulder of an asphalt road.

They paused as a lone automobile raced past. Wilson raised his weapon and aimed it at the receding vehicle, sighting along the plastic barrel. He squeezed the trigger, feigning the recoil which didn't come.

"I still say I won," he said.

"You're dead, Wilson," Cope said.

Matt made no effort to take sides. He gazed across the road

in the direction of a ridge. The crest of the ridge seemed to him like a mirage, an oasis of green rising out of the barren sand flat.

"Wil-son." Matt spoke the name in two distinct parts.

"Yeah?"

"We'll fight the battle over."

Wilson was puzzled. Wasn't it Matt who had said it was too hot? Wasn't it Matt's idea to quit and go home?

Cope was a little surprised, too. He didn't say anything, though it was obvious he was less than enthusiastic about giving in to Wilson—not to mention the heat and the fact that his throat was so dry he couldn't even spit.

"I thought it was too hot for you," Wilson said.

"We ain't going to fight here," Matt said. He lifted his weapon and used it to point across the road at the ridge. "It's cool up there. And there's a well pump we can drink at."

Cope frowned. "Up there with the dead people?"

Matt nodded. "Why not?"

"Yeah," Wilson said. "Why not?"

"I don't know," Cope said.

"Let's go," Wilson said.

"It's okay," Matt said.

The crest of the ridge was a burial place for the poor and homeless. The graves were arranged at all angles amid the unpruned trees and unmowed grass. Some of the markers made of wood were badly rotted. Others of limestone were weathered black and tilted backward or sideways. Inscriptions were barely legible. A few of the graves had sunk into the ground, leaving hollow depressions.

Near the center of the field stood a giant banyan tree. It was to this tree—with its enormous canopy of green supported by a thick trunk and a legion of slender columns—that the three boys made their way. Its huge opaque shadow offered cool relief from the heat. Here, also, was the old well pump. As the boys drank, a whisper of a breeze rustled the leaves of the great tree.

"I told you it was cool up here," Matt said.

"You been here before?" Wilson asked, peering into the crater of a sunken grave.

"Once or twice maybe."

Wilson jumped into the grave and stomped down hard with both feet. "Anybody home?" he hollered, grinning.

Cope's face twisted in disgust. "What the hell are you doing, Wilson?"

"It's only a dead beggar."

"That don't make no difference," Cope said. "It ain't right."

As before, Matt abstained from the dispute.

Wilson laughed as he stepped out of the grave. "I ain't scared of no dead beggar."

Matt walked to the edge of the ridge, to a spot where he could see across the asphalt road to the sand flat where he and the others had played earlier. It glistened like a mirror, the heat shimmering above the glassy surface. He turned and inspected the terrain on the opposite side of the ridge. The ground sloped toward a swamp and in between lay dunes and thickets of saw grass and palmetto.

"I thought we come here to fight a battle," said Wilson.

Matt slipped his arm through the sling of his weapon. "You ready?"

"Ain't I *been* ready?" Wilson replied, his white teeth glowing between sunburned lips.

Matt made the plan. Wilson would stay at the banyan tree and count to one hundred while Cope and Matt found concealment among the palmettos and dunes below the ridge.

"There's some big dunes," Matt said. "Me and Cope will get behind one and wait. And be careful," he cautioned, "there's swamp down there."

Wilson spat on the trunk of the giant tree. "I ain't scared of swamps," he said.

With Cope trailing behind, Matt made his way down the slope. Wilson began counting, slowly at first, his eyes following the boys all the while.

Matt and Cope sat behind a sand dune that was crowned with saw grass. Behind them lay the swamp, its shore bordered by clumps of cattails. Through a notch which Matt had formed by parting the saw grass, the boys could see another large dune several yards away. Like theirs, the dune was covered with saw grass, some of it several feet high.

Separating the two dunes was an oval-shaped patch of black earth. It was peculiar to the rest of the terrain not only in color but in texture as well. Its perfectly level surface appeared dry and crusty and was etched with cracks, resembling a thin layer of mud after the sun has baked out the moisture. Matt had led Cope around the edge, being careful not to set foot on the cracked surface. Cope wanted to know why they just didn't cut across the patch of black earth.

"Nobody can," Matt replied.

The air was dead still under the relentless heat of the sun. From time to time, Matt peered through the notch. Cope was sweating. His mouth was starting to get dry again. Then, without saying anything to Cope, Matt rose from his sitting position, exposing his torso above the saw grass.

"Why you doing that?" Cope demanded in a hoarse whisper. "You want Wilson to see us?" Then he, too, stood up in order to keep from raising his voice. Before he could say another word, though, the tall grass on the dune across the way suddenly parted.

It was Wilson, red-faced, swinging his plastic rifle in a wide arc before him, his voice croaking a guttural imitation of a machine gun.

"You're dead!" he cried. "You're both dead!"

Then, in a gesture of victory, he held his weapon above his head and leapt from his perch atop the dune onto the oval-shaped patch of black earth. His feet exploded through the cracked surface, sending up a watery plume of thick, black muck.

Cope groaned.

Wilson was thrashing about in the black ooze, trying to free himself. But with every attempt to thrust out with an arm or leg, he felt himself sinking deeper. His face lost its redness and was now a ghostly white.

"Quicksand!" he called out in panic-stricken earnestness. "Matt . . . Henry. . . . Help me!" It was the first time Wilson had called Cope by his first name.

Cope slid down the embankment and skirted the patch of black earth until he was as close to Wilson as he dared go.

Matt did not move. He watched the drama of the scene— more like a spectator at a movie or a play. He was interested but detached. In fact, if either Wilson or Cope had the presence of mind to notice, they would have seen that Matt was smiling.

"You ain't afraid of nothing!" Matt finally hollered. "Remember?"

"I'm sinking!" Wilson pleaded. "For God's sake, I'm sinking!"

Cope couldn't understand why Matt hadn't moved. "You got to do something!" He knelt and stretched out his hand.

"I can't . . . reach it, Henry." Wilson felt a rush of despair. Then, ever so gently, his feet touched bottom.

At the water pump in the shade of the great banyan tree, Wilson removed all his clothing. The sun, though it was now low in the sky, had begun to draw the moisture from the black muck that covered most of his flesh. While Matt pumped, Wilson washed each piece of clothing, handing them to Cope who laid them on the grass to dry. Then he crouched under the spout—with Matt still pumping away—and let the cool water spill over his body until the black muck lay beneath his feet, a vanishing pool in the lush grass. Finally, he stretched out beside his clothes and welcomed the sun's warmth. His clothes were still damp when he put them on, but he knew they would dry as he walked.

"Damn," Wilson said as he finished tying a shoelace. "I lost my gun in that stuff."

Matt laughed. "Yeah, but you won, didn't you?"

Cope laughed too. "Ain't that the truth," he said.

They were halfway across the sand flat before another word was spoken.

"That ain't a bad place back there," Wilson said. "It's a lot better than where we usually go."

"Yeah," Cope said. "It's a good place to go when it's hot."

Squinting, Matt turned toward the sun. It hovered just above the horizon, casting a warm, pink glow on the white sand flat.

Gordon Korman

When I was growing up, there really *was* a news story about a guy who was eating a bus. And while my parents found it pretty funny, I was enthralled. I couldn't understand why this Herculean feat didn't dominate every single headline and newscast.

"Hamish Mactavish Is Eating a Bus" started when I looked back and tried to understand why such an odd stunt had so captivated me back then.

No, I don't have a twin brother. I'm an only child, so there's a lot of made-up stuff in there too. But the remarkable attempt to eat a bus unfolds exactly as it really happened. Or at least, as I remember it. . . .

Hamish Mactavish Is Eating a Bus

It was over the Sunday paper that I first learned that a forty-one-year-old man named Hamish Mactavish of Inverness, Scotland, was eating a bus.

The Sunday paper was a family thing at the Donaldson house. Mom and Dad dreamed it up as a weekly ceasefire in the war between me and my worst enemy on earth, that waste of bathroom tissue, my brother, Chase the Disgrace.

Chase and I are twins—not identical, that's for sure. I can't believe we once shared the same womb together. It's all I can bear to be in the same town as the guy, let alone the same house, and three of the same classes. Mom said she experienced a lot of kicking during pregnancy. My theory is that all that action was me trying to strangle Chase with the umbilical cord. I've always been blessed with a good dose of common sense, although I'm not very smart in a school-ish way. Chase got all the academic ability—not to mention the athletic talent, good looks, popularity, and the bigger room, with a view of the mountains, not the garage.

Neither of us could have eaten a bus. That might be the only area Chase didn't have it over me.

"I don't understand why you two can't make a better effort to get along," our mother was always complaining.

Of course *she* didn't understand. She was lucky enough to have been born an only child. She would never accept that we were natural enemies: Lion and antelope; Macintosh and IBM; matter and antimatter; Warren and Chase.

So naturally Chase jumped all over me when I found that tiny little story squeezed between brassiere ads in the wilds of page G27.

"Get out of here!" Chase scoffed. "It's impossible to eat a bus!"

"It's not impossible for Hamish Mactavish," I told him. "He's already half-done with the front fender. So there, pinhead."

"Doofus," Chase countered.

"Idiot."

"Look who's talking—"

"*I'd* like to know how he's doing it," my mother said quickly. "Surely the man can't chew metal and glass."

"I bet he's just eating the body," my father put in. "I mean, nobody could eat a differential."

I held up the short article. "It says here that he cuts the chassis into bite-sized pieces with a hacksaw and swallows them whole. Then the natural acids of his stomach break them down." I turned to Mom. "Can that happen?"

"Over time, I suppose so," she replied dubiously. "This Mactavish fellow certainly must have a strong stomach."

"Strong? He's amazing!" I exclaimed. "I can't believe this didn't make the front page, with a big picture of Hamish Mactavish with what's left of the bus. This guy should be famous!"

"Star of the insane asylum," put in Chase.

I couldn't wait for the six o'clock news. I was positive Hamish Mactavish was going to be the top story. Instead it was something boring about the president. The *president*! I mean, what had he ever eaten? Not so much as a rearview mirror!

Hamish Mactavish wasn't the second story either. Or the third. In fact, he didn't make the news at all. I figured they were waiting for the late-breaking developments to come in over the wire from Scotland. I switched over to CNN, and watched the entire broadcast.

I could hear Chase in the next room laughing at me over the phone on his nightly calls to eighty-five of his nearest and dearest friends. "Yeah, he's been glued to the tube for three and a half hours! Man, talk about stupid. . . ."

And when I went to bed that night, bug-eyed from staring at the TV, I still hadn't heard a single solitary word about Hamish Mactavish.

Kevin Connolly and Amanda Pace were talking about last night's Bulls game when I slipped into my seat next to them in social studies class.

"Michael Jordan was unbelievable!" Amanda raved. "He scored forty and still had enough rebounds and assists for a triple double."

"Yeah," I agreed. "That guy's the Hamish Mactavish of basketball."

"The *who* of basketball?" Kevin asked.

"Don't tell me you've never heard of Hamish Mactavish!" I exclaimed in disbelief. "He's *only* the top-ranked bus eater in the world today!"

"Bus eater?" echoed Amanda.

"He eats buses," I explained. "At least, he's eating one now."

"How much money does he get?" inquired Kevin.

I stared at him. "How should I know?"

"It's important," argued Kevin, who wouldn't even bother to breathe unless he was getting paid for it. "If I was going to eat a bus, I'd expect my agent to cut a monster deal, with a big signing bonus, and a six-figure payoff when I was done."

"He's not doing it for the money—" I began.

But how did I know that Hamish Mactavish wasn't getting paid for his amazing feat? After all, a bus wasn't an extra slice of pizza that you ate because you were too lazy to wrap it up and put it in the refrigerator. It wasn't even like the time Chase swallowed a caterpillar to impress Leticia Hargrove so she'd like him and hate me. This was *huge*!

"Maybe some rich guy is offering a million dollars to anyone who can eat a bus," Kevin speculated. "Or maybe the Scottish government is running out of dump space. They'd pay big bucks to get rid of out-of-use vehicles."

"I think it's more like the Olympics," I told him. "You don't get paid for the actual thing, but afterwards you clean up on endorsements."

"What kind of endorsements?" Amanda asked dubiously.

"Stomach medicines," I suggested. "Can't you picture the TV commercial? 'Hi, I'm Hamish Mactavish. If you think *you* get heartburn, you should see how much eating a bus can upset your stomach. So when a windshield wiper is giving me nausea, I reach for the instant relief of Gas-Away. . . .' "

Kevin looked thoughtful. "I wonder what kind of contract he'd get for that."

"Not as good as Michael Jordan," mused Amanda.

"Don't be so sure," I put in. "I mean, there are hundreds of basketball players. But if you want a guy who can eat a bus, it's Hamish Mactavish or nobody."

I could tell this made a big impression on Kevin. "What a great negotiating position!" he remarked. "Does this Hamish guy need a manager?"

Amanda looked at me with a new respect. "You know, Warren, I never thought of it that way—" Suddenly she tuned me out.

I craned my neck to see what had captured her attention. She was looking at Chase the Disgrace. Chase never just walked into a room; he *made an entrance,* usually surrounded by a couple of his caveman buddies from the football team.

"Hey, Chase."

"What's going on, Chase?"

"What's happening, man?"

My brother slapped his way through the forest of high-fives until he was standing over me. "Are you still babbling about that bus-eating geek?"

The whole class burst out laughing. Not that his comment was so brilliant, or even hilarious. Most of the kids had never even heard of Hamish Mactavish and what he had set out to do. That's just how it was with Chase. He was the big shot, the cool guy, the sports hero, Mr. Popularity. Everything that came out of his mouth was an automatic gem. The football jerks were practically in hysterics. They had to pound each other on the back just to keep from choking.

Most painful of all, Amanda was laughing too, and gazing worshipfully up at my brother's slick grin.

I could feel the crimson bubbling up from my collar until it had taken total possession of my face. "He's not a geek," I muttered tight-lipped.

"Hi, Amanda." The Disgrace shifted his attention to the desk next to mine. "We're going to hit the mall after school. Feel like meeting us?"

If I was Hamish Mactavish's son, maybe people in our school wouldn't be so impressed by a big phony like Chase. I mean, Amanda practically bit off her tongue promising that right after school she'd run home and get her bike. But, then again, if I was a Mactavish kid, Chase would be, too. And he'd *still* be better than me at absolutely everything.

That really burned me up. Even in my own fantasy, I couldn't get the best of Chase. In a rage, I stood up and threw my pen at him as he high-fived the rest of the way to his desk. The ballpoint whizzed past his shoulder and landed in the fish tank. Chase wheeled and bounced a pencil sharpener with deadly accuracy off my nose. Chase was also a star pitcher during baseball season.

"Let's take it easy on the brotherly love today," suggested Mr. Chin, as he set his briefcase on the desk. "Now, this morning I promised we'd talk about the oral presentations. This semester the subject will be your hero, or the person you admire most. It can be someone you know, or even a figure from history. Warren Donaldson—" Suddenly, the teacher's sharp eyes were on me. "This will be fifty percent of your grade. I think you'd bother to take a few notes."

Scattered snickers buzzed through the room. I snuck a look over at the bottom of the fish tank, where the algae eater was nuzzling my pen.

"That's okay, Mr. Chin," I announced. "I already know who my subject is going to be."

*   *   *

It wasn't easy doing research on Hamish Mactavish. There must have been some kind of media blackout over in Scotland. There was nothing about him in any of the papers, and the radio and TV news programs were all about senators, and murderers, and embezzlers, and people who got killed in sewer pipe explosions.

"When are you going to face facts?" Chase taunted me. "Nobody cares about Hamish What's-his-face except you!" The doorbell rang. "Oh, that must be Amanda. We're going to the mall."

"The guys who *built* the mall didn't spend as much time there as you two," I snapped at him.

Amanda poked her head around the corner and waved. "Hi, Warren."

I buried my face in my Hamish Mactavish scrapbook and pretended to be too busy to reply. In reality, I still had only the one tiny article from between the brassiere ads—with fifty percent of my social studies grade hanging in the balance.

Did I give up? Would Hamish Mactavish have given up? Never!

The computer database in our school library found another piece on Hamish Mactavish. Okay, it was from fourteen years ago, and I had to go to the public library to get it—not the branch library near where we lived, but the main building downtown. But I was psyched. Even the forty-five-minute train ride couldn't dampen my enthusiasm. I had unearthed another piece of the puzzle that was Hamish Mactavish.

It took all four research librarians, including the chief, who was about ninety, to find what I was looking for. My hands were shaking as I opened the June 1983 issue of *U.K. Adventurer* magazine. It turned out that my Hamish Mactavish, then twenty-seven, became the toast of the British Isles when he ate a grand piano, bench and all. It was an awesome achievement, but, I now knew, just a training mission for bigger and better things to come.

I squinted at the small picture of Mr. Mactavish, who was posed with a napkin around his neck, and the final piano key in his mouth. He was a pretty weird-looking guy, with wild, almost bulging eyes, and a dazed expression. He was mostly bald, but several long strands of jet black hair hung down his forehead like jungle vines. He also seemed a little on the fat side, with rosy apple cheeks. I guess pianos are pretty high in calories.

Just looking at him, it came to me in a moment of perfect clarity: A guy like that would *have* to eat a bus if he expected to get any attention in this world! Especially if he had to compete with people like Chase.

The chief librarian gawked over my shoulder. "Good Lord, what kind of creature is that?"

"A role model," I answered without hesitation.

"I don't understand why you didn't go to the mall with Chase and Amanda," my mother nagged me.

I was absorbed in pasting the second article in my Hamish Mactavish scrapbook. "They didn't want me," I said without looking up.

She stared at me. "Yes, they did. They *asked* you to go!"

"They were lying."

Mom shook her head. "What is the problem between you two?"

"We have irreconcilable differences," I said stubbornly.

She folded her arms in front of her. "What irreconcilable differences?"

"We hate each other," I told her. "You can't get more irreconcilable than that."

"Open your eyes, Warren," she insisted. "Who put Vicks VapoRub in Chase's toothpaste? Who poured ketchup on the cat the day Chase was trying out his new BB gun? Who called the police and reported the car stolen the day of the big tennis championship so we all got arrested, and Chase missed his match? Poor Chase doesn't hate anybody! It's you who have declared all-out war on your brother, who has never done anything to you!"

"He's done something to me," I shot right back. "He's done a lot of somethings to me. Every time Chase draws a breath it just points out how much more brains, talent, good looks, and athletic ability he has than I do. Compared to all that, I'd say I'm pretty innocent!"

At that moment, the side door flew open, and Chase bounded into the kitchen—*in his underwear*! "I'll kill him!" he seethed.

Mom's eyes bulged. "Where are your pants?"

I looked casually out the kitchen window. Chase's bike leaned against the garage, with his jeans still attached to the seat. I struggled to contain the smile that was crystalizing inside of me. I had applied just the right amount of Krazy Glue.

Best of all, Amanda was nowhere to be seen.

"Good thing he took off his pants instead of ripping them," Kevin said at school the next day. "Otherwise your parents would probably make you pay for a new pair."

"It still would have been worth it," I assured him. "You should've seen the look on his face. It was like the day he threw that big interception with three seconds to play."

Loyal brother that I am, I've never missed one of Chase's football games. Of course, I always sit in the Visitors bleachers and root for the other team. I can usually work the opposing fans into a pretty good chorus of:

> Chase! Chase!
> He's a disgrace!
> Knock that ugly face
> Into outer space!

My family spent a lot of time trying to figure out how all the other teams seemed to develop the same chant.

"Hi, Kevin." Amanda slipped into her seat. She gave me a dirty look.

I know I should have been upset. But I just couldn't shake the image of Chase riding up to the mall beside Amanda, and then trying to get off his bike. He had probably struggled a little—imperceptibly at first, then with increasing effort until his front tire was bouncing up and down on the pavement.

AMANDA: What's wrong, Chase?

CHASE: Uh . . . just checking the air in my tires . . . (more bouncing, becoming violent)

Kevin sensed the tension and decided to change the subject. "I've been thinking of some marketing angles for Hamish Mactavish. How about this: A coast-to-coast bus trip where he actually eats the bus in different cities as he goes along. He could roll into the L.A. Colliseum on just the motor and four wheels, and scarf down the chassis in front of fifty thousand screaming fans. I call it 'The Hamish Mactavish Disappearing Bus Tour.' "

"It doesn't work that way," I replied. "He has to cut everything into small pieces and swallow it. It takes months."

"Oh." Kevin seemed disappointed. "Well, how about a TV miniseries, then? Or we could set up a hotline, 1-900-EAT-A-BUS, and charge people three bucks a minute to hear him talk about how—"

I didn't catch the rest because my chair was yanked out from under me, sending me crashing to the floor. Rough hands grabbed me by the collar, and I was yanked to my feet by two of Chase's football linemen. Hot breath from their bull nostrils took the curl out of my hair.

"Let him go," muttered Chase.

"Come on, take a punch!" I egged him on. "I'd rather lose all my teeth than owe anything to the likes of you!"

"Don't push your luck, Warren," he warned as he took his seat, followed by his two goons.

I concentrated on Amanda. She was now staring at Chase with *twice* as much admiration and adoration as before. I guess he'd been wearing his very best underwear yesterday. Unbelievable.

To make matters even worse, Mr. Chin was trying to get me to change my topic for the oral presentation.

"I know you're disappointed, Warren," the teacher told me. "But I really don't see that there's enough material available about the man for a whole term assignment."

"I know that," I defended myself. "That's why I wrote Mr. Mactavish a letter. I'll bet he can send me tons of information."

Mr. Chin frowned. "How did you find his address?"

"Oh, I just put Inverness, Scotland, on the envelope," I replied airily. "After all, how many Hamish Mactavishes could there be?"

"Mactavish is one of the most popular names in Scotland!" he exploded. "Hamish Mactavish is like being named Joe Smith over there!"

"Oh." My face fell. "I just figured it was taking him a long time to get back to me because he was so busy, what with eating a bus and all."

The teacher sighed. "There's still time to choose a new topic. I think you'll have no trouble finding someone a lot more admirable than a wild eccentric who's doing something silly."

I leaped to my feet, feeling the hairs on the back of my neck standing on end. "It's not silly," I protested. "Don't you get it? Hamish Mactavish is a total loser. He's fat, he's ugly, he's not too bright—if there's anyone with a good excuse to throw in the towel in life, it's him. But he didn't! He found the one thing he can do that's absolutely unique! Okay, it's a crazy, stupid thing, but it's *his* crazy, stupid thing, and nobody can touch him at it! And in a world where Hamish Mactavish can hit it big, none of us are ever hopeless!"

I sat down amidst the laughter and jeers. Spitballs and erasers bounced off of me. People were whistling inspirational music, and playing imaginary violins. In one short speech, I had cemented my position as the class joke. Even the teacher wore a big grin, although he was trying to hide it.

In fact, the only nonparticipant in this party at my expense was Chase, who sat staring straight forward, his expression inscrutable. Still mad over the Krazy Glue thing, I guess.

It was the night before the oral presentations were set to begin. All in all, a pretty ordinary night at our house except that Chase had wrangled the best spot on the couch, so I was crammed into the corner with a lousy view of the TV.

". . . and finally," the news anchor was saying, "the latest word from Inverness, Scotland is that Hamish Mactavish has given up his bid to eat a bus. According to the forty-one-year-old Mactavish, he was having trouble digesting the tires."

The sportscaster started to make some kind of a wisecrack, but I was already running for the stairs.

"Warren—" my father called.

I burst into my room and slammed the door. I couldn't believe it was all over. Just like that. One minute something special, *historic* was going on, and I was part of it. The next I was nobody again.

I don't know why I felt so betrayed. Hamish Mactavish didn't owe me anything. Who was I to talk? I wouldn't even eat broccoli, let alone seven tons of metal and glass and rubber.

There was knock at my door. "Warren, open up."

It wasn't my folks. It was Chase the Disgrace, probably to rub salt in my wounds.

"Get lost," I snarled.

"I'm really sorry, Warren," Chase said from the hall. "I know how much Hamish What's-his-name meant to you."

"He's a quitter!" I rasped.

"He made an amazing run," Chase amended. "Nobody could have come as close as he did."

It hit me right then: Fighting with my brother got on my nerves, sure. But Chase actually being *nice*—that drove me absolutely insane!

"Leave me alone!" I bellowed. "Go call Amanda! Go be the star of the world!"

Calm down, I told myself. My heart was pounding in my throat. This was 50 percent of my social studies grade, and I was poised to flunk in spectacular style. I had until morning to think up another subject—like Sting, or maybe Harriet Tubman. Then the plan was to get down on my knees, howl at the moon, tear my hair out, and beg, plead, entreat, and cajole Mr. Chin to please, please, *please* have a heart, and give me an extension!

"I knew he couldn't do it," Kevin greeted me in class the next morning.

"Shut up, Kevin," I yawned, bleary-eyed from a sleepless night. "You were ready to send the guy on a coast-to-coast publicity tour!"

"Not anymore," he replied. "His marketability is permanently damaged. I couldn't book him into a grade-school cafeteria, let alone the L.A. Colliseum. You know what our mistake was? The Scotland thing. Why should we go to some foreign country for our superstar? There's plenty of talent right here at home. If we searched the Midwest, I'll bet we could find some farm boy who could eat a combine harvester on national television. Now *that's* American."

Mr. Chin breezed into the room, and I immediately put my plan into action. "Sir? Could I have a word with—"

"Later, Warren," he cut me off. "I want to get started with the oral presentations. Who would like to be first?"

Normally, no one would volunteer, and the teacher would have to pick somebody. But this time there was a hand raised in our social studies class. Most amazing of all, it belonged to Chase the Disgrace. I couldn't believe it. My brother would *never* put his image on the line and be first at something.

"Ah, Chase," the teacher approved. "Go ahead."

As Chase walked to the front of the class, I checked out Amanda. Instead of staring at my brother in nauseating rapture, she was looking over at me! What was going on here?

"Most people think of heroes as winners," Chase read from his notes, "but I'm not convinced that's always true. It's no big deal to pick up a basketball if you're Michael Jordan, or to do something you know you're going to be great at. What's a lot harder is to try something even when the odds are stacked up against you. Sometimes failing is more admirable than succeeding. . . ."

It all clicked into place in a moment of exquisite agony— Chase's sudden kindness last night, his volunteering to go first, Amanda watching me, not him. After a lifetime of beating, outperforming, and besting me in every imaginable way, Chase was delivering the final *ultimate* insult. He had figured out a way to do his oral presentation on Hamish Mactavish when I couldn't. He was even better than me at *being* me!

The dam burst, and white-hot blinding rage flooded my brain. *"Why you double-crossing—"* I leaped out of my chair, and made a run at my brother, with every intention of leaving this class an only child.

"Warren!" Mr. Chin stopped me a scant six inches from Chase's throat. "Have you lost your mind?" He held me by the shoulders, his face flushed, but not half as red as mine must have been.

"You're the lowest of the low!" I seethed at Chase. "You're the slime trail of the mutant parasites that crawl around the sludge of the toxic waste dump!"

"Warren, go to the principal's office!" ordered the teacher.

Chase stepped in. "Please, Mr. Chin, let him stay. I want him to hear this." He returned to his notes, and continued his presentation. "The person I picked isn't always successful, but he's heroic because he never gives up when a lot of us would. When *I* definitely would. That person is my brother Warren."

There are times in this life when you feel like the biggest total moron in the galaxy, but you just have to stand there and take it, because anything you say will only make things twenty times worse. My jaw was hanging around my knees, as Chase went on about my strength of character and my resilience; how others fell to pieces when the cards didn't come up aces, while I was always ready to do my best with the two of clubs.

When he finished, all eyes in the class were on me. And for the first time ever, I couldn't think of a single rotten thing to say to Chase the Disgrace.

"This doesn't mean I like you," I managed finally.

He stuck out his jaw. "You either."

"Of course, you're not such a bad guy," I added quickly.

"We're brothers," he replied with a grin. "We've got to support each other."

I pounced on this. "Switch rooms with me?"

"In your dreams!" laughed Chase.

"Pinhead."

"Doofus."

"Idiot."

"Look who's talking—"

Well, at least I was his hero. That was a start.

Walter Dean Myers

The Incident:

When I was a kid at Stuyvesant in New York I met a black girl from Brazil who worked at Hubert's Flea Museum as an exotic dancer. She was really down on her luck and had to keep the two snakes she used in her act in the kitchenette she rented. The snakes were kept in a box with two lightbulbs in the box for warmth. I went out with her once and when we returned the electricity in her room had been cut off and the snakes had died. At the time I was fifteen and completely self-absorbed. She was at loose ends and older—I really don't know how much older. I want to believe she was really going to Columbia.

Sunrise Over Manaus

Sometimes you find life swirling around you like dead autumn leaves. You move through it and you hear its rustle and you think you're making progress but you really aren't. All you're really doing is making the noise of life, making yourself heard so that at least you know you're there if nobody else does. That's the way things were going for me when I first met Elena Alacar Cabrera.

At the time I was about two inches and a phone call away from being kicked out of high school. It was my fault, I knew that. I wasn't doing the work and whenever a teacher or the principal said anything to me I had to come back with some kind of wisecrack. It didn't come as a surprise that the teachers didn't like my remarks, but I couldn't give them up. Then one day a teacher just stopped in the middle of the class and told me to shut up. I got up and walked out of the class.

"And where do you think you're going, Mr. Simms?" he asked.

"Out of your life, Blue Eyes," I said.

Then I walked. Out of the classroom, down the stairs, out of the building, and into the official world of Trouble. It was as if I had a momentum going, a flying head start toward disaster and I couldn't stop. Somebody started figuring that I had some kind of psychological problem. It had something to do with some tests I had taken to get into the Magnet School. I had creamed the exam and they were thinking I was some kind of near genius or something. So it was natural to ask that if I was so smart why was I acting like such a jerk. Glad they didn't ask me, because I didn't have a clue.

They called my mom and said I had a choice. I could transfer to what they called an Alternative School or I could go to a city clinic once a week for counseling. That's how I found myself down at the Community Service Outreach Center.

The first visit was okay, maybe even interesting. I took some tests and had what they called an Intake Interview. The guy giving the interview asked me a lot of questions about what I liked and what I didn't like, and what I read—stuff like that. He said he wouldn't be my counselor but that I would like the person assigned to me.

My first counseling visit was on a Wednesday at four-thirty. I got to the center at a little past four but I had a book, *Père Goriot,* to read so everything was cool.

The clinic was more or less depressing. The walls were a dirty ochre and the dark mahogany benches looked like something out of an old black-and-white movie.

I had just opened the book to my place when she came out of the office. She was tan and tall and kind of thin, with large, sad eyes that glanced nervously up and down the gloomy corridor. She sat on the bench a little way from me and I saw that she was crying. She was sniffling, pulling her head back as if the crying had already escaped her body and she was trying to bring it back inside. But the thing you noticed most, I mean you didn't stare or anything like that, but you had to notice, was that there was a sense of despair about her.

I fished in my backpack and found some tissues. I took the top one off because it was pretty grungy, and handed her the pack.

She looked at me and reached for the tissues. She blew her nose and offered the unused tissues back to me and I held up my palm to signal that she could keep them. She sat there crying the whole time I was waiting to go in and I sat there like a dummy staring at the page in front of me and not being able to read a word of it.

Finally this woman comes out and calls me in. She calls me William, and then she asks if she can call me Bill. Bill? Yo, lady, I said to myself, my name is James, James Simms. What chart are you reading?

"Sure, you can call me Bill."

I sat at her desk and she went through a whole thing about how smart I was and how much potential I had. Nothing new. How did I get along with people? How did I get along with my parents? Did I ever feel hostile to my classmates?

My answers were mostly true. Only mostly true because sometimes it's hard to figure out just how you get on with somebody. I mean, if I knew how other kids got along with their parents then I could tell if the way I was getting along was okay. The forty minutes went by really fast and she was saying how she would see me the same time the following week.

"And is your name William or James?"

"James."

"Oh." She gave me this puzzled look and wrote something down in her notes.

The next week I got there at four-fifteen and the counselor, her name was Miss Easter, told me to come right in, that her three-thirty appointment hadn't shown up.

We went through the same thing about how smart I was and then her asking me, in this real calm voice, why I thought I wasn't doing better.

"Because I'm really the devil in disguise," I said.

"Really?"

Really? It was supposed to be a joke. Lighten up, lady.

The session ended with Miss Easter asking me how I would feel having the next session with my mother.

"I think it might be useful," she said, smiling with her eyes more than with her mouth.

"I think the idea sucks," I said.

"Then perhaps another time," she said. Same smile. Same calm voice.

The clinic has a coffee shop and I stopped in it for a candy bar and the girl I had seen last week was sitting by herself in a corner. She had a cup on her table and the place was fairly crowded. I got the candy bar and a can of soda, then went over and asked if I could sit at the table.

She looked at me and I think she was about to say no when she recognized me and nodded.

As soon as I sat down I went into a mild panic. What was I going to say to her? I looked down at the soda and at the table, my usual smooth approach. When I looked up at her she was looking at me and I figured she wondered why I was sitting there.

"She say anything about me?" I asked.

"Who?" she asked. She moved her head back and to one side like maybe she was leery of me.

"Miss Easter," I said.

"Why are you seeing her?" She had an accent that sounded something like Puerto Rican and something like West Indian.

"I have to come here because I got in trouble in school," I said. "It's either come here or get into real trouble. My fault, mostly. How about you?"

She shrugged and looked away. "I got trouble, too," she said.

"What school do you go to?" I asked.

She didn't answer. We sat there a while without saying anything and I took a bite out of the candy. Around us in the cafeteria there were people sitting at the tables, poor people mostly, some of them looking like maybe they were homeless and had just wandered in to get away from the cold.

"My name is James Simms," I said. "The school checks to make sure I come here once a week."

"My name is Elena," she said. "Elena Alacar Cabrera. I'm from Brazil and I'm supposed to be going to Columbia University. Do you know Columbia?"

"Yeah, sure," I answered. "You say you're supposed to be going to Columbia—that mean you're not going?"

Her eyes misted over and I thought she wasn't going to answer at all. Her hands moved in front of her, as if they were starting the conversation by themselves.

"It's too hard to live here," she said, her voice trailing away so that I had to lean across the Formica-topped table to hear her. "Having a job, going to school, it's just too hard."

"Columbia's tough," I said. I had dreamed of going to Columbia and majoring in English Lit, but there was no way I would ever get in, not with my grades.

She looked up at the clock on the wall, said she had to leave to go to work and started gathering her things.

"Where do you work?" I asked.

She didn't answer, but took out a pen and wrote down an address on Forty-second Street. As I looked at it she was already walking away.

It was a little past six by the time I got uptown to Harlem. When I got home my Mom had an attitude, something about my father never taking her anywhere. That's what my life was about, not going anywhere, only where my Mom was drifting along, not going anywhere in a slow way, I wasn't going anywhere in a big hurry. Maybe that didn't make sense to anyone but me, and sometimes it didn't even make sense to me, except when I said it I knew that's how it felt.

It wasn't until a week later, on a Thursday evening, that I took the local train down to where Elena worked.

What I thought was that she worked at one of those small shops that sold everything for under a dollar or maybe a fast-food place. Forty-second Street was crowded when I got there. There were some tourists just kind of wandering around looking at New York like they expected something weird to come out of the sewers, a whole bunch of dudes standing in the shadows waiting for something to happen, and rushers. Some of the rushers were working, trying to get some place in a hurry, others weren't working, and I figured they were just anxious to get away from someplace they didn't want to be. I could understand that.

The address that Elena gave me was a games arcade. A sign in front of the place said GAMES! GAMES! GAMES! in bold black letters and under that, in smaller green letters, something about Hubert's New Flea Museum. I walked in and looked around and didn't see Elena so I asked a guy who was making change. He grunted and pointed toward a staircase.

"You need a ticket," he said. "A dollar."

"I'm a friend of hers," I said.

"You need a ticket. A dollar."

I paid him the dollar, gave the ticket to an old guy standing at the top of the stairs, and went down into the basement.

The stairs led to a fairly large, well-lit room. There was a small stage and a bored-looking woman with tattoos all over her body was standing on it. A guy stood next to her and talked about her tattoos.

The woman on the stage was old. The tattoos on her arm sagged with the skin and her thin legs were white and fragile. When the crowd started looking away, the announcer guy started clapping for the tattooed lady and she left. Then the guy announced the Amazon woman who danced with snakes.

The doorway on the stage wasn't really a door but a curtain and as soon as the brown arm came through it I had a feeling it was going to be Elena. It was. She came out wearing a bathing suit with feathers stuck in it and she had sandals on her feet. The dark snake around her shoulders looked dead until she held its head up. The announcer went to a tape recorder and pushed a button and the room was filled with the sound of low drums as Elena started to dance.

She couldn't really dance. She moved from place to place on the stage, holding the snake above her head or near her face as if it was very dangerous. Elena didn't see me at first, she kept her eyes fixed over our heads, shutting us out.

A tall blond man said something in what sounded like German to a woman next to him who craned her neck forward to look at Elena.

Eventually she did look at us, only a handful of people, mostly men, staring at her. When she saw me she looked quickly away and I was embarrassed for her. I wanted to run out and somehow never have been there. But it was too late and I stayed until the announcer turned off the tape recorder and started talking about a man with skin that stretched clear over his head.

"You'll be frightened and disgusted!" he boasted.

I waited for Elena upstairs and wondered if she would leave a different way. When she showed up she didn't say anything to me, just stood next to me.

"I've got two dollars left," I said. "You want to go someplace for coffee?"

"Do you like Brazilian coffee?" she asked.

"I guess so," I said.

She didn't live far. Hubert's New Museum was on Forty-second Street and she lived on Forty-eighth between Eighth and Ninth avenues, across from the firehouse.

My house wasn't great or anything. I mean, me and my folks lived in a two-bedroom apartment in a so-so neighborhood, but Elena lived in a place that was the deep pits. It was called The Cort and the halls were dark and smelled like somebody had sprayed stuff around to cover up the way the place stunk. It didn't work.

One flight up a guy hunched over a newspaper behind the counter. He wore a faded New York Giants T-shirt that left a gap of four inches between its bottom and his belt. He reached for a key and handed it to Elena, all the time keeping his eyes on me. On a stool behind him there was a metal bar with one end taped.

"Why are you going to the clinic?" she asked after she had filled a pot with water and put it on the little two-burner stove that sat on a counter. "Are you sick?"

"I don't know," I said. "I don't think so. I'm just kind of drifting. You know what I mean?"

She shrugged. "What do your parents think?"

"They've got answers. They always have answers. I heard my dad saying that I was going through a phase," I said. "What about you? What do your parents think?"

"My parents are in Manaus," she said. "They think I'm studying to become a doctor. Then they think I will come back to Brazil and take care of them."

She took a bag full of coffee and poured some of it into the pot. I never saw anyone making coffee like that before.

"So why are you going to the clinic?"

"I hurt myself," she said in this real quiet voice. "And the hospital gave me an appointment."

You could see the hurt. You could feel the weight of it around her.

She poured the coffee and asked me if I took milk and sugar and I said no. It was sort of a macho thing because I saw this guy in the movies take his coffee black. Actually I figured it didn't much matter because I didn't like coffee anyway.

"How old are you?" she asked.

"Seventeen," I said. I was big enough to be seventeen. "You?"

"Seventeen," she said.

"So, what are you going to do?" I asked.

She looked down into the coffee like maybe she was going to see something in the cup.

"In my country, in my city of Manaus, I lived near the ocean. I always knew what to do there. Sometimes on weekends I would take my books and start off before daylight. There was a small hill and I could climb it and wait for the sunrise and sing to it. I loved to see the sun spreading over Manaus, and the way the city would come to life slowly."

The room was small. The light from the one bulb in the middle of the ceiling didn't reach the corners. On the dresser a small white candle flickered gently in its red glass holder. Behind it stood a painted statue of Jesus on a silver crucifix.

Quiet again. The silence pushed in on me, found me out. Where were my wisecracks now that I needed one?

"That's a nice cross," I said. Stupid thing to say.

"My father gave it to me on the day I left Manaus," she said. "He said if I took care of Jesus then He would take care of me."

I asked her if she knew what time it was and she shook her head no. It had to be close to midnight and I wanted to leave. I felt tired and drained. It wasn't any big deal for me to stay out late, but I didn't want to hear my mom's mouth. We sat for a while and a couple of times I thought Elena was going to cry again.

"How did you hurt yourself?" I asked.

Her mouth tensed and she moved her left hand off the table and onto her lap. I sat for a while longer and then started buttoning up my jacket.

"Thank you for coming," she said, seeing me preparing to leave.

"I'll see you around," I said. "You coming back to the clinic?"

"I don't think so," she said.

"Well, like, so long."

She stood, then turned quickly and went back to the dresser. She cupped the candle with her hand and blew out the candle, then took the cross and handed it to me.

"Would you like this?"

"No," I said.

"It's Jesus," she said, looking at me like I had to want Jesus.

I took the statue and put it halfway in my pocket so that the crossbar and the top of Jesus was sticking out. The guy behind the counter stared vacantly at me. He looked dumb enough to be scary.

Outside it was cool enough for the air to smell good, even in New York. There were a few characters around, leftovers from the night before, and a few of them looked toward me. They didn't say anything, just kind of looked as if maybe they wanted to see what I was. Not who, for most of them looked as if they had lost their identity a long time before, but what.

Elena had overwhelmed me. She was in it deep. She seemed all right, probably smart, but her problems were like tremendous and the kind where you couldn't think of anything to do. I had a picture of her in my mind riding a bus into some small neighborhood in Brazil and everybody waiting for her to produce a diploma.

A gray-haired woman with a cane came up to me on the uptown local. I thought she wanted a handout and I started to look away when she spoke.

"I like to see a young man who is right with the Lord," she said.

I pushed Jesus deeper into my pocket.

My mom was up and she went into her "I'm-not-going-to-say-a-word" act. This was usually followed by her asking me if I wondered why she was so quiet and I would have to say yes and then she would spend an hour telling me how words failed her.

I walked over to where she sat and put the crucifix right in front of her. That shut her up.

The bed felt good and I was half asleep when I realized that I felt all messed around inside. When Elena's father had given her the cross she had said that if she took care of it then it would take care of her. Now she had given it to me.

In a way I kept thinking that me and Elena were a lot alike. On the subway home I had even imagined taking walks with her and holding her hand, stuff like that. But as I lay there in the dark I knew we were different. I wasn't going anywhere with my life but Elena was someplace. Her people were putting all kinds of faith in her and were counting on her to do something to help them. I wasn't looking to help anybody or even thinking about helping anybody. The thoughts I had were bad, but there was one thought that was even worse. Elena had been given the cross for her own protection, and now she had given it away. I thought of how her mouth had moved when I asked her how she had hurt herself.

My jeans were draped over a chair and I snatched them off

and jumped into them. My keys were on the dresser and I snatched them up with my left hand as I pulled a sneaker on with the right.

Mom had turned in and I didn't see the statue. I tied my sneakers on good and went toward my parents' bedroom. They were talking and I knocked on the door.

"Jimmy?" my mother's voice called.

I opened the door, saw the statue on the chest at the end of their bed and snatched it up.

"You in a cult?" my dad asked. "You'd better tell me if you're in a cult."

On the way out of the room I turned the light off.

The train took forever to come. All I could think about was Elena not having the statue, and what she might do because she didn't have it. Pits.

Two dudes who looked like they were scoping the platform for somebody to rip off looked me over, saw the statue, and moved on. Thank you, Jesus.

It took sixteen minutes for the train to reach Forty-second Street. Up the stairs and along Eighth Avenue. A light rain had started and the cars hissed along the street and neon signs did a kind of shimmy on the street corners. I slowed to catch my breath when I got near her block.

The front of The Cort was dark and the front door was locked. I knocked on the glass a few times and then noticed a bell. I rang it and nothing happened. I rang it again and again until I saw the guy who had been sitting behind the first floor counter bent at the waist, stumbling down the stairs to see who was ringing. He had the pipe in his hand. When he saw it was me he waved me away and started back up the stairs again.

I pushed the bell again and again and he came down the steps and opened the door, puffing himself up and making motions with the pipe like he was going to hit me.

"If I have to stay out here ringing the bell all night I will," I said.

"You get yourself out of here before I call the police," he said, spitting as he spoke.

I put my foot in the door and he tried to kick it out.

"I'm calling the police," I said. "You let me in or I'll get every cop in New York on your case."

He looked at me and I knew he wasn't sure what I was going to get the police for. Neither did I, but it looked like it might work.

"There's a girl in trouble," I said. "And if I can't get in to help her I'm getting the cops and they'll get in."

"No overnight guests," he said. He said it like it was what he was supposed to say and had just forgotten it before. "No overnight guests."

"I'm not staying overnight."

He moved away from the door and I pushed past him and hit the stairs running. I could hardly breathe I was so scared. The guy who let me in was a step or so behind me but he stopped at the top of the stairs and peeked around the banister to see what I was going to do.

I knocked on the door, once softly and then loudly.

"Elena, it's me, Jim."

I heard a noise inside, or maybe I thought I heard a noise, and I banged on the door again.

"What you doing?" the hotel guy called to me from the stairwell. He was getting his nerve up again.

There was no way I could stand up against the guy, especially with him holding a pipe and I thought I was going to have to leave when the door opened. The chain was still on and Elena looked out at me.

"It's me, Jim," I said.

She closed the door and I heard her taking the chain off. I turned toward the guy with the pipe and threw him a salute.

Elena had been crying, her eyes were red and swollen. On the dresser the candle was still lit and there was an open Bible next to it. Next to that was a razor blade.

"You have to. . . ." I wanted to say something cool to her about taking care of the Jesus statue or maybe taking care of herself, but I was so filled up with being glad that she hadn't hurt herself the way I thought she would, and the way she might have, that none of the words came out right.

"You're crying," I said.

Her face was a mess and I took a towel off her table and wiped her tears away.

She put her head against my chest and her arms around me and started sobbing. I didn't know what to do. Mostly I just stood there with my cheek laying against the top of her head for a long time.

When she stopped crying she took the statue from me and put it back in its place. There was an old wind-up clock on a chair and I saw it was a quarter past six.

"It's going to be daylight soon," I said.

"Go home and sleep," she said. "I'll be all right."

"Not sleepy. Maybe I'll just go for a walk."

She picked up her coat, it was too thin for the weather, and went out with me. She had to stop to use the bathroom in the hallway. I hadn't even noticed that her room didn't have a bathroom.

"No overnight guests!" the guy with the pipe said as we passed. His heart wasn't in it.

We walked up Eighth Avenue until we got to Central Park. The morning sky had lightened and in the distance I could see a small streak of orange.

"What was the song you used to sing to the sunrise?" I asked.

"It's a Portuguese song," she said. "You wouldn't understand the words."

"I'd still like to hear it."

She kept walking close to me then stopped and looking right into my face started singing a soft little song that sounded like the kind that children sang. She was right, of course; I didn't understand the words, but I didn't care.

When she had finished singing we sat for a while on a bench. Whenever I would try to say something she would put her fingers to my lips to quiet me.

We watched the sun come up and I imagined her watching the same sun come up over her hometown in Brazil. I guess it had meant a lot to her, having that sun come up and knowing that it would bring a whole new day, a whole new beginning. When you gave it some thought it really seemed something to sing about.

"Thank you for bringing Jesus back," she said. "It was wrong of me to give Him away."

"Yeah, well, I guess I know how you felt," I said.

Elena and I hung out for two more weeks before she got enough money to go back to Manaus. I liked hanging out with her and I thought maybe we could get into something, like a boyfriend-girlfriend kind of thing, but she didn't want any part of that. That was okay with me, too. Not that I wouldn't have liked a girlfriend, but I did have, for those two weeks, somebody I cared for that wasn't wearing my sneakers. What happened was that I discovered her. She was like Manaus, distant and foreign when I first saw her, and she was becoming real. Okay, so I took a day off from school to go to the airport with her and it was crazy and sad saying good-bye to her. But she left me with the feeling that there were other people to be discovered, and that was real good.

It was a full three months after she left before I heard from her again. I got a package from her. There was a letter in it that thanked me for being her friend and saying how she was working in a bank and maybe next year she would go to a

school in Brazil. She said she had learned a lot in New York
and had made one very good friend. She said that she had sent
me something to take care of. In the bottom of the package,
wrapped in a dark blue cloth, was a small crucifix.

I still didn't get a handle on school, but I managed to get by
and to keep my mouth shut most of the time. It wasn't that I
had learned anything, there just wasn't anything that important to say.

Joan Lowery Nixon

When our son Joe was in his early teens, we lived in a small town in Texas. Joe had a doctor's appointment for a routine booster shot, and he insisted he was old enough to go to the doctor by himself. No parents or older sister needed or wanted. Maybe Joe was right. Maybe I was being overprotective. Maybe there was nothing to worry about. I allowed him to make the office visit by himself.

But Joe came home subdued and shaken—and just a little scared. An elderly man had come in with a relative and had taken a seat directly across from Joe's. Slumping with seeming exhaustion, the man waited for his turn to see the doctor. Finally, a nurse called the man's name, but he didn't respond.

"Wake up, Uncle James," the woman with him said. But Uncle James didn't wake up. He was dead.

No Matter What

I heard the jangling crash of a bicycle being thrown on the front walk and jumped to my feet. I couldn't count how many times Mom and Dad had told my ten-year-old brother Danny, "Don't treat your bike like that! Take care of it." I was in charge of Danny while Mom and Dad were at a sales conference in nearby Midland, so, as Danny burst through the front door and stumbled into the room, I snapped out the same words.

Danny, his dark hair tousled, stared at me through huge, frightened eyes for only a split instant, then whirled to slam and lock the front door behind him. Every freckle on his face stood out against skin so pale it seemed translucent. "Megan," he whispered, "I gotta talk to you."

"Danny! You look awful! What's the matter?" I cried.

Danny didn't answer. He clapped his hands over his mouth and dashed into the hallway. I heard the bathroom door slam and the sickening sounds of violent retching.

I sighed impatiently. It wasn't easy taking care of a ten-year-old brother, not even for a weekend. He didn't like my being in charge and wanted to argue, argue, argue over everything. The last time I had given up—probably too easily.

"You're too young to go to the doctor by yourself," I'd insisted.

"I am not," he'd complained. "Mom made the appointment. It's just a follow-up because of my sore throat, and she promised that I won't be getting a shot." He looked away, a little embarrassed. Everyone in the family knew Danny's fear of needles and shots.

"I can take care of myself," Danny said. "I don't need a bossy big sister to tag along after me."

"It's hot and sticky, and the wind is filled with dust. I can drive you."

"You think you're a big shot, Megan, but you only got your license a few months ago. Besides, I can ride my bike."

I thought about the street traffic, about weirdos—yes, even small towns have them—about Danny getting lost, and about Mom emphasizing my responsibility in taking on this job. But Danny's lower lip stuck out as he said, "If you try to go with me, I won't go," and I gave up.

"Okay," I shouted. "Go by yourself. Who cares?"

Now, everything Mom had told me came back in a king-sized guilt trip.

"Megan," Mom had said, "you're only sixteen. Are you sure you can do a good, thorough, competent job of taking care of Danny, no matter what?"

Impatiently, I'd rolled my eyes. "Relax, Mom," I'd said. "Trust me. I can take perfect care of Danny . . . no matter what."

How could I know what "no matter what" covered? I realized that even though Danny had complained, I should have gone to his doctor's appointment with him. I hung outside the bathroom door, a glass of water in my hand.

In a few minutes I could hear tap water running and guessed that Danny was probably washing his face, so I knocked lightly at the door. With all my heart I wished Mom was on hand. She'd know what to do. "Is your sore throat worse?" I asked. "Did the doctor give you something that's making you sick? Should I call the nurse?"

The door opened, and Danny leaned against it. He zeroed in on the glass of water and took it from me.

"Sip, don't gulp," I cautioned.

"Megan, stop telling me what to do," Danny said. He took a long, slow drink, then added cautiously, "Don't call the nurse. You might get the wrong one."

"How can there be a right or a wrong one? There are only three nurses."

"Four."

I knew there were only three, but I wasn't going to quibble. "And they all work for Dr. Lee."

Color began to come back into Danny's face, and I stopped worrying about him, but there were still some things I needed to know.

"What happened to make you sick?" I asked.

Danny's face closed in, as though he were seeing something no one else could share, and a gigantic shudder shook him from the top of his head down to his toes. He began to cry.

I took the glass of water out of his hands, placed it on the floor, and wrapped my arms around him, holding him tightly as tremors shivered through his body. He was terrified of something.

Holding him off, trying to look into his eyes, I asked, "What is it, Danny? What's scaring you?"

He wiped his eyes and nose on one sleeve, leaving a long, wet smear. "An old man came into the doctor's waiting room," he said. "He sat in the chair right across from me." Danny shuddered again, then said, "He's dead."

"Oh, Danny, how awful!" I told him. "How did he die?"

"He was just sitting there. And then the nurse with the dirty laces on her shoes came by."

"Dirty laces? Nurses don't wear dirty shoelaces."

Danny's lower lip trembled, but it rolled out stubbornly. "I know what I saw. Her shoelaces were dirty."

He paused, and I put an arm around his shoulders, pulling him close. "What else did you see?" I asked.

He shivered, but didn't answer.

"Did you see the man die? Is that what's frightening you, Danny?"

Danny pulled back so he could look up in my face. "I didn't know he was dead. I thought he was asleep. Sarah called his name—"

"Sarah? Dr. Lee's receptionist?"

"Yes." Danny took a deep breath. "The man didn't answer, so the woman who was sitting next to him said, 'Wake up, Uncle Frank.' And then she kind of screamed. And then she hollered at the receptionist, 'I think he's dead!'"

Danny had told me his story, yet his body was as tense as a string on Dad's guitar. There was something more that was bothering him. "What else do you want to tell me?" I asked.

Before Danny could answer, the doorbell buzzed loudly, and we both gave a start.

"Don't answer!" Danny whispered and grabbed my arm.

"Don't be silly, Danny. I have to see who's there," I said.

Danny groaned again and dashed into the bathroom, locking the door.

The door buzzed again—this time a long, insistent buzz. I sighed and answered it.

A tall, slender man, with thick brown hair and a smattering of freckles across his nose, stood on our front porch. "Miss Sanderson?" he asked.

"Yes," I said.

"You have a brother named Daniel Sanderson?"

"Danny? Yes."

"Are your parents at home?"

Mom had taught me what to say to strangers. "They're due home any minute."

The man wore jeans, a dark cotton shirt, a jacket, and spotlessly clean white running shoes with cream-colored laces. He reached into the inner pocket of his jacket and pulled out a small leather folder. He opened it and quickly flashed the contents in front of me. It looked like a business card and a metal badge, but everything happened so fast I couldn't read what was written on either of them.

"Detective Bart Ridgway," he said. "Sheriff's Department. May I come inside and wait for your parents?"

"No," I said. "If you're with the Sheriff's Department, why aren't you wearing a uniform?"

"Plainclothes detail," he answered. He looked at me for a moment, as though sizing me up, and said, "Is your brother home? I'd like to talk to him."

I didn't budge. "Why should he talk to you?" I asked.

"Because it's important that I contact him before anyone else does," Ridgway said.

"Why?"

Ridgway sighed impatiently. "Okay. I'll tell you what I can," he said. "Have you ever heard of Frank Berkeley?"

"Everyone in town knows about Frank Berkeley," I said.

I'd heard Mom and Dad talking about Mr. Berkeley. According to local gossip, the man was terribly rich. Probably a billionaire. He was in his mid-nineties, and his nieces and nephews were already arguing about the money he was going to leave them. Mom said she heard that one of them was even trying to get Mr. Berkeley to change his will.

Ridgway said, "This morning, because Berkeley had suffered painful leg cramps during the night, his niece Julia took him to see his doctor—Dr. Lee."

"Surely, he didn't die from leg cramps," I said.

"You know that Frank Berkeley's dead." Ridgway gave me a piercing look, and I blushed with embarrassment.

"Yes, Danny told me."

"What else did he tell you?"

"Nothing much. Just that the receptionist called Mr. Berkeley's name and he didn't answer, and his niece tried to wake him up and couldn't." I thought of telling Ridgway what Danny had said about the nurse with the dirty shoelaces, but I changed my mind. It sounded dumb.

"Did your brother happen to mention any unusual circumstances regarding Mr. Berkeley's death? We have reason to believe he saw what took place."

It took a moment for everything he'd said to register. The shock of surprise hit me like a blow to my stomach. "Are you talking about murder?" I asked.

Again the searching look before Ridgway looked at his watch, then back to me. "Please ask your brother to talk to me," he said. "It's very important."

"I'll ask him," I promised and shut the door. Murder? Danny hadn't said anything about a murder. And, yet, I was positive that Danny hadn't told me the whole story. He hadn't had a chance.

Shakily, I walked into the hallway and called, "Danny, there's a policeman here to see you," but Danny didn't answer.

I rattled the knob on the bathroom door. It was locked. "Danny, open up," I said. "You don't have to talk to the policeman if you don't want to, but at least come out of there.

No answer.

I ran to the kitchen and got a small screwdriver—the one Dad had always used when Danny was little and accidentally locked himself in the bathroom. I poked it into the little hole under the handle and jiggled it and the handle until the door opened.

The bathroom was empty, and the window over the toilet was wide open.

"Oh, Danny!" I said aloud, terrified that he had run and I didn't know where he was. "What did you see? What do you know?"

The steadily blowing wind already had deposited a sifting of gritty dust along the sill, so I automatically reached for the bottom of the window to pull it down and close it. But Ridgway's voice stopped me.

"Where's your brother?" he demanded.

I whirled to face him, gasping with fear. "How did you get in? The door automatically locks."

"Those automatic locks are nothing. Fortunately, you forgot to fasten the dead bolts."

"You're with the Sheriff's Department," I said, "so you know that it's not legal to break into people's houses, even for the police."

"This is an emergency," Ridgway said. "I told you. It's important that I reach your brother before anyone else does."

"Important to who? You?" I challenged.

"To your brother," he answered. He looked through the bedrooms until he found the messy room that was obviously Danny's. Ignoring me and my protests, he searched under the bed and in the closet.

Finally, back in the living room, Ridgway faced me. "Do you know where he's gone?"

"No," I sobbed. I was surprised to discover that I'd been crying.

Ridgway opened the door, but I grabbed his arm. "What is this all about?" I asked. "Does it have to do with murder?"

His glance was so sharp that I winced. "Murder?" he asked. "If it was, it's going to be nearly impossible to prove. That's where your brother comes in. He was the only eyewitness to Berkeley's death."

"D-Danny d-didn't say anything to me about a murder," I stammered, but I thought about how terrified he'd been and how I was sure he hadn't told me everything he'd wanted to tell.

"We tried to question him, but he bolted," Ridgway said. He pulled an envelope from his jacket pocket, tore off an end and wrote a phone number on it. Handing it to me, he said, "If you find Danny, or if he comes home soon, please call this number. It's very important that I hear what Danny has to say."

I'd seen enough cop shows on television to know that this didn't seem right. "Don't you have a business card?" I asked.

"You've got the phone number. That's all that's important," he said. Without another word he strode across the porch and cut across the lawn to his car.

I didn't watch him drive away. Danny's bike was gone, and I had a fairly good idea of where he'd taken it.

As I was about to close the door a marked car from the Sheriff's Department pulled up to the curb in front of our house. Two men in uniform got out, came up the walk, and handed me their IDs. They gave me plenty of time to read them.

"Is your mother home?" the one named Thomas asked.

"My parents are out of town," I answered.

By this time they stood right in front of me. "Your name, please?" Thomas said.

"Megan Sanderson."

"Do you have a brother named Daniel Sanderson?"

"Yes."

"May we speak to him, please?" the deputy named Scott asked me.

I said, "Look, Danny isn't here. I don't know where he is, but he got scared and took off when your Detective Ridgway came to question him about what he saw in Dr. Lee's waiting room."

"A person named Ridgway questioned him?"

"Bart Ridgway, your detective. But I told you, he didn't get to question Danny. Danny ran away."

They looked at each other. "There's no one in the Sheriff's Department named Ridgway," Scott said. "Suppose you tell us about him."

My stomach clutched as I described Bart Ridgway and told the Sheriff's deputies what we had talked about. Finally, their questions stopped, and I asked, "Who is Bart Ridgway?"

"That's what we're going to find out," Thomas said. "In the meantime, I'd suggest you think of anyplace your little brother might be hiding and let us know."

I was afraid to put my question into words, but I did it. "Do you think that somebody's after Danny because he might have seen Mr. Berkeley's murder take place?"

Again they glanced at each other before studying me. "Who said it was a murder?" Scott asked.

"Mr. Ridgway," I said.

Thomas gave me a business card. "You can reach us at this number," he told me.

It wasn't until after they'd driven off and I'd locked and

bolted the front and back doors, that I realized I was still clutching the scrap of paper with Ridgway's phone number on it. Why hadn't I given it to the deputies?

Shrugging, I tucked the paper into the pocket of my jeans. It didn't seem important now. The only thing I had in mind was finding Danny. And I thought I knew where he might be.

I needed Mom. I needed Dad. I put my hand on the phone, ready to dial the number they'd left for emergencies, but I waited, not knowing what to tell them. I couldn't say, "Come home. A murderer is after Danny. He's run away. I'm going to try to find him." They'd be so unstrung, they'd probably have an accident on the way home.

I shuddered. What could I tell them? Nothing that made sense. I'd have to try to handle this myself, no matter what.

I'd learned about Danny's secret place one day when I'd been practicing my driving on traffic-free streets and had wandered into a block north of town in which a builder had planned a community of homes. It was during the oil boom of the early eighties and he'd named his development Brushwood Point. But suddenly the boom had busted, as people said in West Texas. The big companies left town, and with them the employees who could afford large, beautiful homes. Ever since then, three partially built houses on Brushwood Drive have sat alone on oversized lots, ragged and dusty, like sightless, eroding monuments to another world in another time.

I had spied Danny's bike lying on a front walk, so I'd parked Mom's car and done some exploring for myself. In back of the house I'd found a door with a hole cut for hardware that hadn't been installed. The door was ajar, so I'd silently entered. And it was there, in a dim wood-paneled room, that I'd discovered Danny in a fort he'd built out of old lumber scraps.

"How'd you find me?" he'd yelled indignantly.

"If you're going to hide, then don't leave your bike in plain sight," I'd said and laughed. "You've got a good fort here."

"I've even got ammunition," he'd said, and pointed to a pile of dull chrome knobs, and what Dad calls elbow joints for pipes. There were even a couple of showerheads.

"Don't tell anybody, Megan! This is my secret!" Danny had begged me, and I promised I wouldn't. Everyone needs a private place. When I was Danny's age my private place was in a closet with a louvered door. I'd perch on a pile of luggage and play with my dolls in utter contentment, because no one in the whole world knew where I was.

Now, I knew where Danny had gone. He had to be hiding in his fort.

I headed for the garage with my driver's license and a ten-dollar bill tucked into my hip pocket, and Dad's cellular phone hooked to my belt. I eased Mom's old gray sedan onto the street and forced myself to take off slowly, just in case someone was watching.

Someone was.

I had driven only a block before I realized that I was being followed by a sedan as nondescript as Mom's old clunker. It was staying a good block behind me, so I couldn't get a good look at either the car or the driver. I raised, then lowered my speed, and the car stayed with me at the same pace. I turned down a block, then down another, and the car followed.

The forgotten, unfinished houses on Brushwood Drive were nearby, so I headed into the parking lot of a large supermarket. Leaving the car, I walked into the front door of the supermarket and out the back.

A guy who was busy tearing outer leaves off a box of heads of lettuce looked up as I passed by. "Hey! You're not supposed to be here," he said.

"It's okay. I'm leaving," I told him, and walked down the open ramp that led to the alley. I cut through to another boulevard, crossed it, and followed a path through residential streets to Brushwood Point.

There was no sign of Danny or his bike. With trembling fingers I eased open the back door to the house in which Danny had built his fort, and tiptoed inside. As I saw his bike resting against the frame of a kitchen counter, I sighed with relief.

I quietly walked to a spot near the door of the library. The house creaked and snapped in the heat of the day, and I could imagine ghostly figures trailing down the stairs and up my backbone.

Shivering, I whispered hoarsely, "Danny?"

Something crashed near my head, bouncing off the door frame. I picked up a showerhead and yelled, "Cut that out, Danny! It's me—Megan!"

Danny's head slowly rose over the battlements. "Megan!" he cried shrilly. "Get in here! Hurry! They might be coming!"

"*Who* might be coming?" I asked.

"C'mon! Hurry!" Danny insisted.

He visibly trembled with fear, so I quickly leaped over the barricade and crouched down. I dropped the showerhead and put my arms around him.

"You shouldn't have come here. What if somebody followed you?" he asked.

"No one followed me," I said. "I made sure of that."

For a moment I stroked his shoulder and arm, trying to soothe him. Then I asked, "Danny, tell me exactly what you saw in Dr. Lee's waiting room."

"I told you most of it."

"Tell me the rest. You wouldn't tell the Sheriff's deputies, so tell me."

"I couldn't tell them, Megan. The nurse with the dirty shoelaces was there. She pulled me outside. She said she was going to give me just a little shot, and I wouldn't feel a thing. But somebody else was coming."

I held him tightly. "That's when you ran, wasn't it? You must have been awfully scared."

"I was. I didn't want to die, too."

"Did you think that the shot would make you die?"

Danny nodded vigorously. "It made Mr. Berkeley die."

I tried not to show the shock I felt. Quietly, I asked, "Danny, what did you see? How did Mr. Berkeley die? You can tell me."

"He was sitting in his chair, looking at a magazine in his lap," Danny said. "Some people came in the room, and some people walked around, looking for chairs. Sally told everybody that Dr. Lee was running late, and the waiting room was filled with people. A nurse came in with a lot of magazines and handed them out. Then another nurse came in, only she came from outside. She went around behind Mr. Berkeley, and bent over him for just a second. I saw a needle. She gave him a shot in his neck." Danny's voice quavered, and a tear rolled down his cheek. "She saw me watching her. Megan, I didn't want her to give me a shot in my neck, too."

"Of course you didn't," I said. "And she won't. Not ever." I hoped Danny wouldn't hear the fear in my own voice. "What did Mr. Berkeley do after the nurse gave him the shot?" I asked.

"He went to sleep, I think," Danny said. "He put his head down on his chest, and he stopped reading his magazine." He shuddered. "But then the woman with him said he was dead."

"What did the nurse look like?" I asked.

Danny looked up at me, surprised. "A nurse," he said.

"I mean, did she have dark hair? Or blond? Or gray? Was she short or tall? Thin or fat?"

Danny thought a long moment. "She had dirty shoelaces," he said.

I put a finger up against his lips. I'd heard creaking steps at the back of the house.

My heart hammered so loudly in my ears I could hardly hear Danny's whisper, "Someone's here."

I glanced around the windowless room. This wasn't a fort.

We were in a trap! The steps came closer, and I froze, unable to move.

Bart Ridgway stepped into view and smiled at me. "You were easy to follow," he said. "It's a good thing you found your brother for me."

"Megan, look at—" Danny whispered.

"Now I can take care of him . . . and you," Ridgway said. His smile grew broader.

Danny clutched my arm, the pressure of his fingers painful. "See . . . the dirty shoelaces," he whispered.

I took a good look at Ridgway's shoes. His white running shoes were a brilliant, brand-new white, but the laces on his shoes were cream. Up against the white, they did look strange. I guess to Danny's eyes the darker color seemed dirty.

It was then I noticed the glass syringe and needle that appeared in Ridgway's hand. Danny did, too. I could hear him suck in his breath.

"You were the nurse who injected Mr. Berkeley?" I asked.

"I was, complete with uniform and wig." He chuckled, looking smug, as though he wanted to brag about himself.

The fingers of my right hand closed around the shower head I'd dropped.

"The will had been changed, and someone wanted to make sure it stayed that way, so they hired the best."

"You're a hit man?" I whispered.

"It doesn't matter who I am," he said. "By tonight I'll be in another state, unrecognizable to anyone in this town, and you . . . well, you and your brother won't be around either." He raised the syringe. "This will drug you until I decide what to do with you."

I jumped to my feet and threw the showerhead, aiming at the syringe. It was a good hit. The glass shattered, and I could see little pinpricks of blood appear on Ridgway's hand and wrist. He and I both stared as they blossomed like flowers.

"What have you done?" he screeched. He stared at his hand and at the puncture marks where the fluid had entered his body. Then his eyes rolled back and he flopped like a rag doll to the floor.

"Is he dead?" Danny whispered.

"No," I said. "He'll wake up in a few hours. I pulled Dad's phone from my waist and Thomas's card from my pocket and made the call.

I told Thomas what had happened, and where to find us, and said, "The charges are murder, attempted murder, and—oh, yes—breaking-and-entering. Danny and I are eyewitnesses."

Thomas told me that he and Scott were on their way, so I hung up. I glanced again at Ridgway and was awfully glad he was going to wake up in jail.

"Mom," I planned to say, "you asked me to do a good, thorough, competent job of taking care of Danny, no matter what. The *no matter what* was the hard part, but hey, look! I did it!"

Richard Peck

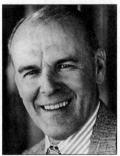

All writing is moving from one experience to another, from reading to writing. Still, there are people who think we writers have to *live* our stories before we can write them, that fiction is real life with the names changed. We want more credit than that for imagination, and for being readers ourselves.

No one arriving at my house was ever killed on the way, but turned up anyway so lifelike that I didn't know he was dead. I don't even believe in ghosts, but ghost stories have been told around campfires forever. Notice the fire burning in the hearth in my story. The greatest play ever written begins with the ghost of Hamlet's father. Ghosts are in the grand tradition of storytelling.

Never think I'm trying to improve on Shakespeare. In *Hamlet*, though, there's a play within the play, and in my story there's a story within the story: the tale Ben tells of the maiden invited to share the knight's lonely exile because he died before he could love. Is this what happens to Melanie? Weirdly, it would seem so.

I never even had a daughter I had to beg to stay home with her brothers, but the world is full of nine-year-old boys who think they're too old to need babysitting. We writers reach for our readers where they live, hoping to lead them into the wider world of storytelling. And we are inspired by other storytellers. Nobody but a reader ever became a writer.

The Most Important Night of Melanie's Life

When Melanie suspected she'd have to babysit her brothers, she made a fine plan to be over at April's house. She and April were best buds. Melanie had listened on the extension to hear her mother talking about the party she and Dad would be going to. It was a business thing, wives included. So Melanie was ready when her mother mentioned it.

"Absolutely not. I have to be at April's. It's only the most important night of my life."

"What's happening at April's?" her mother asked.

Nothing was planned. April hadn't even sounded that happy about Melanie coming over, so Melanie said, "Mother, if you keep prying into my private life, I may have to go on drugs or something. Do I have to account to you for every minute? I'm fourteen."

So her mother offered her the going baby-sitter rate with ten dollars on top to sweeten the deal.

Melanie turned her down flat. "It's a matter of principle. If I start baby-sitting the boys, you and Dad will be going out every month or so. I won't be a teenager. I'll be your slave. The twins are only nine, and the baby's seven. They're going to need sitting for years. I'll be an old woman by then."

Melanie knew she'd won when her mother sighed, "I sure miss Trish." Up till last summer they could count on Trish from next door, but now she was away at college. "I guess we'll have to find somebody else."

"Do that," Melanie said.

Then the boys put up an argument. "Hey, we don't need a sitter," the twins, Mike and Mark, said. "Give us the money, and we'll sit Clem." Clem, the seven-year-old, said nothing but looked pained that anybody thought he needed any supervision. "We're way too old for a baby-sitter," Mike and Mark said. "Add our ages together, and we're eighteen."

Then they found out the baby-sitter was a guy. They didn't know him. His name was Ben, a nephew of the Hutchinsons three streets over, visiting.

"What kind of guy baby-sits?" Melanie said, rolling her eyes.

"One who likes kids," a twin said.

"And money," the other one said.

Then they heard he was sixteen. "Wow," the twins said. "He'll be in high school."

"Cool," Clem said softly.

It was rain turning to sleet that night, and Ben was late. Dad stood in the front hall, jingling his car keys. "We ought to be there now," he said, "and the streets are glazing over." Mom was all dressed up and ready too. Melanie came down the stairs in a stocking cap and her down jacket from Urban Outfitters.

"Honey, we've got to leave," her mother said. "Just hang around till Ben gets here."

Melanie smacked her own forehead. "You've got to be kidding. What if he doesn't show? Then I'm stuck here all evening with these dweebs. No way."

She was out the door, aiming at April's. Dad's keys were jangling like church bells by then. So finally Mike and Mark promised they wouldn't even move till the sitter got there.

When their parents were gone, silence fell over the house.

"It's like *Home Alone*," Mike said in a spooky voice.

"It's neat," Mark said.

Before they could work up a plan, they heard a sound outside. Feet scraping on the welcome mat. When they opened the front door, Ben was there, filling it up. He was definitely high school. He wore a flight jacket, black jeans, ball cap on backwards. Ice crystals gleamed in his sideburns, and his eyes seemed to see farther than a kid's.

"Wow, you sure are tall," Mike said. "How tall are you?" They crowded around him but let him in. He was wearing very big boots.

"You probably drive," Mark said. "Did you drive over here?"

In those first moments Ben's mind seemed far away. "No, I walked," he said, "partway."

"We're Mike and Mark," the twins said. "You can't tell us apart. This is Clem. He's the baby. He's only seven."

Then Ben did a fantastic thing. He reached down and shook hands with all of them, even Clem. So it wasn't like having a baby-sitter at all. Ben's hands were ice cold, but at sixteen you probably don't even have to wear gloves.

In the living room he towered over them, gazing around almost like he was surprised to be here.

"We could run some movies," Mike said. "You ever see *Nightmare on Elm Street*?"

Ben looked down at them. "I've seen something scarier than that."

"What?" Clem said, hugging himself.

"You guys!" Ben said, and they all yelled and started punching each other because Ben was great.

They didn't even turn on the TV. They got out their baseball cards to show. Clem brought out the plastic dinosaur skeleton he'd put together from a kit. They had hot chocolate and a big bag of pretzels. Ben hadn't taken off his flight jacket. He said he couldn't seem to warm up, so they decided to have a fire in the fireplace. He showed them how to lay it and let Clem light it.

They were all hunkered down on the hearth, so now it was

like a campfire. Mike said, "You know any stories? They got to be scary." Ben thought about that, rubbing his chin. He shaved.

"All my stories are too scary for you guys," he said, so they all yelled and pounded on each other until Ben began, "It was a dark and stormy night."

"Heard it," Clem said.

But they got him quieted down, and Ben told a story about a ghost in a tower somewhere in England. In life, the ghost had been a knight, so in stormy weather you could hear his armor rattle.

Clem's eyes got round.

A beautiful young girl came on a visit to this castle, and she started having these nightmares about a suit of armor. It was just a regular suit of empty old armor standing over in a corner. But then in the dream she'd see the finger on one of the chain-mail gloves move. Her nightmare drew her nearer and nearer. Something urged her to release whoever was inside.

Her dream hand came out to lift the visor on the helmet. There within, staring back at her, were the empty eye sockets of an ancient skull. Black beetles glittered in the sockets, but all other life had long fled. Her screams echoed down all the corridors you get in nightmares.

The twins and Clem were sitting closer to Ben now.

The dream returned to the girl until she no longer dared to sleep. One night she threw back the covers of her bed. Wide awake, she was drawn up the turning steps, higher and higher into the tower. Holding a flickering candle aloft, she came upon a heavy door that opened easily. There in the corner stood the suit of armor she'd known from a dozen nightmare nights. She moved nearer. Her hand reached out. Hoping against hope that seeing the skull would rid her of her terrible dreams, she lifted the visor.

Inside the helmet a young man's piercing eyes met her gaze,

but his voice was hollowed by the years. "I died too young, before I could love," he said. "Will you redeem me? Come away to share my lonely exile in a world beyond this one."

Ben's voice died away, and the crackling fire burned low. Clem's eyes were perfect circles. Mike and Mark gave each other a look. It was an okay story until the end.

"Ben, you know any stories without girls in them?" Mike asked.

Then behind them, the front door banged open. Feet stamped out in the hall. The twins and Clem jumped a foot.

Melanie stalked into the living room, jerking at her stocking cap and unzipping her down jacket. "April and I had a major fight. She's such a—"

Ben was climbing to his feet, turning toward her. Melanie froze. "Oh wow," she said, looking all the way up at him.

"I'm Ben." He put out a big hand.

The stocking cap fell from Melanie's hand.

"Hey, Melanie, clear out," Mike said. "We're telling stories. No girls allowed."

"We've been having a great time," Ben said, just to her.

"Yeah," she said in a voice nobody had ever heard from her. "They're nice little boys."

She and Ben were still shaking hands, very slow.

"You're in high school?" Melanie said in this new voice of hers. She seemed to be a bug caught in the beam of Ben's gaze.

"I was," he said.

"Better yet," Melanie murmured.

"You want to go out for a little while?" Ben asked her.

"Hey, no fair," Mark said.

"Why not?" Melanie said. "Before my parents get back." Then in her regular voice she said to the twins and Clem, "You creeps don't even think about getting into trouble, okay?

Like make my day, right?"

Ben reached down, swept up Melanie's stocking cap, and handed it back to her. They turned, very near each other, and walked out of the house without a backward glance.

Silence fell. Mike said, "I knew when he put that girl into the story, things were going to turn out stupid."

The three of them sat slumped before the dying embers of the fire. "What could he see in Melanie?" Mark wondered.

"It's a mystery," Clem said.

They forgot how long they sat there, watching the fire flicker out. Then they heard the sound of the car, and right away the front door banged open again. Their mother and then their dad raced into the living room, coats flapping. They didn't wipe their feet or anything. Their mother dropped to her knees and tried to get her arms around all three of them.

"Are you all right?" she said, gasping, trying to pull Clem closer. "What have you been doing all this time? We just got word from the Hutchinsons."

"Who are they?" Mark asked.

"Ben's aunt and uncle. Oh, it's too terrible. Ben . . . I shouldn't even tell you."

Their mother's hand covered her mouth. "Boys," Dad said, "the reason that Ben didn't come to sit for you tonight is that he had an accident. On his way here, he was struck by a hit-and-run driver. They found his body by the side of the road. He was dead before your mother and I ever left the house tonight."

Now the eyes of all three of them, Mike and Mark and Clem, were all perfect circles.

"And where's Melanie?" their mother asked, looking around. "Isn't she home yet?"

Susan Beth Pfeffer

A lot of times students are told to write a story based on something that happened in their own lives, and they don't know what to write because their lives haven't been all that interesting.

The important thing about fiction isn't to write exactly what happened, but to be accurate about your feelings.

I went to a very small private school from grades one through seven. Eighth grade I transferred to the public junior high school in my town. I went from a grade of seventeen kids to one of four hundred. I was confused, exalted, terrified, and thrilled.

"Young Blue Eyes" is a first-day-of-school story. It may not be exactly the way it happened to me, but I tried to be true to my emotions, if not my eye color (which is green).

Young Blue Eyes

Of course I was homesick. They'd warned me about that lots of times. Be prepared to be homesick, and don't be surprised if you have trouble opening the doors.

You would think such an advanced civilization would have automated all its doors. But it hasn't, and I walked into a dozen doors the first dozen rooms I entered. All the doorknobs were in the center of the doors, and my hand would automatically reach to the left, which is where doorknobs are on Earth. Not that Earth's doorknobs are better. The guidebooks all told me not to assume just because I was used to things being one way on Earth, it meant they were better that way. But I sure did get tired of walking into those doors.

I guess I was expecting more on Zyglot because all my life grown-ups have been telling me how perfect it is there. Or more to the point, how perfect the children there are. "Why can't you be more like Zyglot children?" teachers used to shout at us. "Zyglot children are always so well behaved." Once we had an entire school assembly telling us about the children of Zyglot, and they made this really big point of showing us all those little Zyglotians doing their homework and being polite.

I speak for all Earth kids when I say Zyglot kids were our teachers' dreams and our own worst nightmares.

You may be asking yourself how it was I ended up on Zyglot? A good question, and one I've asked myself plenty of times, especially each time I walked into a Zyglot door.

It was my mother's idea. "Travel is so broadening," she said. You have to understand, Mom's never been farther away from home than the supermarket. But I guess she figured I should do the traveling for both of us. So when I came home from school and told her about the Zyglot Student Exchange Program, she made me sign up for it right away.

Frankly, I never thought they'd pick me. The school I'd be going to had never had an Earth student there before, and I don't think of myself as exactly representative of all that's best in my species. Even my principal was surprised when she heard I'd been selected.

"Well, you're typical enough," she said. "I guess they're looking for someone kind of average."

That's me all right. Your kind-of-average high-school student with a mother who wants to travel through the galaxy, and is counting on me to get her the frequent flier miles to do it with.

After I was picked, they gave me all these orientation lectures, so I'd feel at home right away on Zyglot. Of course there was no way I was going to feel right at home on a planet that insists on putting its doorknobs dead center, but we all had to pretend the orientation sessions were working. One good thing about them. I picked up Zyglotian pretty easily, and except for an accent that cries out EARTH, language hasn't been a problem. And it turns out "Ow!" is the same on any planet. At least everyone on Zyglot knows what I'm saying each time the doorknob and I make contact.

I guess if I'd been born with three arms, I'd find a doorknob in the center perfectly sensible too. They gave me my third arm (robotic, of course; cheaper than the surgically attached kind and almost as useful) about a month before I left home and told me to wear it every day until I was used to it. That's great advice, but if your clothes only have two sleeves, a third arm smack in the middle can be a real nuisance.

At night, I'd take off all my clothes, and put the arm on for practice, but I never did get the hang of it. That's what it did mostly, hang down. And nobody tells you that Zyglot women have breasts about three inches further apart than Earth women, which is why they can manage having a third arm in the center of their chests.

"Earth boys have trouble with the arm too," they told me when I complained at the orientation sessions. "Just give it some time and practice and it'll feel natural soon enough."

Tell you the truth, I would have dumped the arm altogether except that schools on Zyglot all insist on uniforms, and I would have felt pretty silly with that empty sleeve flapping around all day.

So the first few days I was homesick and black and blue, but they put me with a nice family, and that helped. Zyglotian family structure is a lot like Earth, a mother, a couple of fathers, and no more than seven children in each litter. That's a joke, folks.

Anyway, my Zyglotian family consisted of a mother and daughter. I was told to call my Zyglotian mother Em, which is their equivalent of Mom. I would have felt funny calling some stranger Mom, but Em had a nice sound to it. And Em's daughter, my "sister," was named Grudnick. Grudnick's my age, and she couldn't be nicer. Every time I bumped into a door, she'd say how she was sure if she were on Earth, she'd be bumping into doors all the time herself.

I got to Zyglot about a week before school started. During that week, all the Earth kids had a big orientation session at Bruzchok University. I made a lot of good friends that week, since we were all bumping into doors and trying to get our arms to work, and it was comforting being with kids just like myself.

But then the school year began, and we had to say good-bye. Lots of crying and swearing we'd stay in touch, but of course the whole idea of being an exchange student is you don't hang out with other Earth kids. So we each started at the schools we'd been selected for. And if you think I'd felt homesick before, you should have seen me carrying on as we Earth kids said good-bye to each other.

But I'm a resilient kind of person (which may be why they picked me), and first day of school is exciting and scary and fun no matter where you go. Em helped me on with my uniform, and Grudnick swore she'd stick around and make sure I didn't get too lost.

"Be sure to use your arms," Em cried out to me as we began the long walk to school. "The middle one comes in so handy!"

She laughed, so I guess that's like a Zyglot joke. I tried not to hold it against her.

"See those girls up ahead," Grudnick whispered to me as we entered the schoolyard. "That's Marju and Drosis and Hooleete. They're the most popular girls in school."

"The best behaved too, I bet," I said.

Grudnick gave me a funny look. She'd given me a lot of those since I first moved in with her and Em. "Why would you think that?" she asked.

"Because we were always told how perfect Zyglotian kids were," I replied.

Grudnick laughed. "We were always told the same about Earth kids," she said.

Grown-ups. They're the same on any planet.

Anyway, I felt better once I knew I wasn't going to be sur-rounded by hundreds of perfect little Zyglotians. Three arms I might master. Being on my best behavior for a solid school year was a guaranteed impossibility.

"What makes them so popular then?" I asked.

"It's their looks," Grudnick said. "They're the prettiest girls in school, and they know it."

I looked at them more carefully, which was kind of hard, because they (and everyone else at school) were staring at me. "I think you're prettier," I said to Grudnick. I did too.

"Oh no," Grudnick said. "They're real beauties. Look at their eyes."

Which was pretty funny, because for the week I'd been on Zyglot, the one thing I'd been trying hard not to look at was eyes. It had been pretty easy avoiding the eyes, since I'd been spending most of my time looking down at my third arm, will-ing it to behave itself. But the other thing is, there's only so much different you can accept at any one time, and Zyglotian eyes were past my threshold level.

But I figured if they were going to stare at me, I might as well stare back. Grudnick was right about their eyes. Three girls, nine eyes amongst them, each eye a distinctive color.

"They're very pretty," I said, although I didn't mean a word of it. I've got two eyes, myself, both blue, and I have to admit that's how I like it. Of course I used to feel that way about two arms too.

Marju whispered something to Drosis and Hooleete, and they all giggled. I couldn't be sure, but I had the feeling they were laughing at me.

I know they were when I bumped into my first door of the day. Everyone laughed then, except for this one boy.

"Let me help you," he said.

I could tell by Zyglotian standards this guy was a looker. He would have done okay for himself on Earth for that matter. Three big eyes, red, yellow, and green. They sparkled like traffic lights as he smiled at me.

"Thank you," I mumbled.

"I like your accent," he said.

"I like yours too," I said, which was pretty dumb, because he didn't have one. I mean, he sounded just like all the other Zyglotians. But it's hard to flirt when you keep noticing you have fifteen fingers, and you can't quite tell which eye you're supposed to make eye contact with.

He just laughed and walked off. Marju, I noticed, scurried after him. I found Grudnick again, and she led me to my first class, which was Zyglotian History. A subject I happened to be extremely up on, since they'd been shoveling it down my throat since I'd been named an exchange student.

I knew a lot of answers to the questions, and I figured this was a good time to show off, since I only had to raise one arm to get called on. Besides, I figured they'd be pleased I'd learned all that stuff. And I could see the teacher was getting a kick out of me, the Earth kid, knowing the dates and places of important events on Zyglot.

I guess it annoyed the other students though, because after

the teacher had called on me three or four times, I could hear some murmurings. The teacher could hear them too.

"You Zyglotians should be ashamed of yourselves," he said. "This Earth girl knows all about your history. And she's a perfect example of Earth youth. Polite, respectful, and attentive. You should all try to be more like her."

I wanted to say I wasn't at all the way he was describing me, that Earth kids were always being told how perfect the Zyglotian kids were, but it was my first day, and I didn't think it was such a good idea to annoy the teacher. After a while, I was sure he and everybody else on Zyglot would lose their illusions about me.

Besides, it was a kick and a half to be held up to the class like I was some kind of perfect Earth kid. I guess you'd have to have sat through that awful assembly about perfect Zyglotian youths to know how it felt.

The rest of my morning classes I didn't show off though. I'd tried to learn about Zyglotian literature, but there was no way I could hold my own there. And math on any planet is not my best subject. But I did okay, and just as long as the doors were open, I didn't make a total fool of myself.

Not until gym at least. But that was a nightmare.

Back home I'm a pretty fair athlete. My speciality is track events, and I've run some pretty respectable times. But even with two arms and two eyes, my hand-eye coordination isn't the best. It's no big deal. I stick to sports where I don't have to throw or catch things, and I do fine.

Only that day in gym, they were playing Boodlach. Boodlach, in case you missed it during the last Intergallactic Olympics, is the team sport of Zyglot. It's exclusively a middle-arm game. You get penalized if your right or left arm touches the ball. And you lose style points if the ball goes below your forehead, which is where both of my blue eyes happen to be located.

I was the last one picked for the team. Not that I could blame them, but it was an awful feeling as girl after girl was selected and I stood there feeling, well, feeling like the only two-eyed two-armed kid in the school.

Eventually they ran out of other kids, and somebody selected me. I knew they were all hoping nobody would hit the ball anywhere near me.

Of course the other team's entire strategy was to aim the ball my way. Which they did, over and over again.

I tried. I mean, I really tried. I tried holding my right arm with my left one, behind my back, so I wouldn't be tempted to take a swing at it. But it seemed like every time I tried hitting the ball my middle arm was too weak and too late, and the ball kept landing on my nose.

The final score was 128 to 7. That means my nose got bopped 128 out of 135 times.

Lunch followed gym. I took one look at the typical Zyglot school lunch and bolted to the girls' room. They can tell you a hundred times that what you're used to isn't necessarily better, but when you've just made a total fool of yourself and your nose hurts and your chest is black and blue, the last thing you want to deal with is a plate of still-wriggling worms, no matter how good the sauce is.

Luckily for me, and all the other Earth women who find themselves on Zyglot, we go to the bathroom the same way. I found myself an empty stall, and sat down for what I anticipated would be a good twenty-minute cry.

But before I had a chance to let myself go, I heard three girls enter.

"Don't worry, Marju," one of them said. "Tradbeam will never look at her twice."

"Hooleete's right," another girl said. "The way she showed off in history class? He hates that kind of stuff."

"And she was awful in gym," Hooleete said. "I loved how you kept hitting the ball right at her."

"I'm surprised she still has a nose left," Drosis said.

"But the way he looked at her," Marju said.

"It's only because she's new here," Hooleete said. "Trad-beam always flirts with new girls."

"Besides, think about her eyes," Drosis said. "Just two and they're both the same color."

"That's true," Marju said. "She does have the ugliest eyes I've ever seen."

The girls kept on talking, and I kept on hiding. Eventually they left, and when they did, I let the tears stream out of both my baby blues.

I guess I stayed in the girls' room long enough for Grudnick to worry, because after a while she showed up calling for me.

I let myself out of the stall (after bumping into its door).

"You've been crying," she said. She reached out to comfort me with her middle arm.

"I don't fit in," I said. "And I never will. My arms. My eyes." It was all I could do to keep from blubbering again.

"You'll get better with your arm," Grudnick said. "We'll work on it every night. And as far as your eyes go, why don't we just give you a third one."

"What?" I said. I could just imagine what Mom would say when she got the bill for a surgically implanted third eye.

"We'll put it on with makeup," Grudnick said. She took out some eyebrow pencil and outlined a perfect third eye for me. It was about as useful as my third arm, but I didn't care.

"What color do you want it?" she asked.

"Blue," I said, because I hadn't gotten out of the Earth mindset about eyes matching. "No, pink. Do you have pink?"

"Of course I have pink," Grudnick said. She painted the center of the eye a bright pink. It just about matched my red nose.

"Now you look like a Zyglotian," Grudnick said.

I stared at myself in the mirror. I did too. It was a shame two of my eyes were the same color, but except for that and the fact I wasn't bald, I looked just like all the other girls.

"If you want, we can shave your hair off when we get home today," Grudnick said. "Then you'll really fit in."

It's funny. Grudnick couldn't have been nicer. And she was saying just what I'd been wishing for a moment earlier. So I guess it wasn't the arms or the eyes. I guess it was the hair.

But whatever it was, I knew right then that no matter what Grudnick did, I wasn't going to fit right in. Not if I pretended to be a Zyglotian for the entire school year.

"No," I said. "I'm from Earth and everyone might as well know it."

"Your hair means a lot to you, doesn't it," Grudnick said.

Of course it did. I'd brought a year's worth of shampoo with me. But that wasn't what decided me.

It was the thought of all us Earth kids being taught Zyglot kids were perfect. And all the Zyglot kids being taught the same thing about us.

I was on Zyglot to show kids what Earth kids were really like. It was possible one day one of the kids I was in school with would hold major political office on Zyglot, or be involved in intergallactic trade with Earth. And they had to know what Earth people, real Earth people were like. Two eyes and all.

"It's a lovely eye," I said, tearing off some toilet paper and wiping it away gently. "Thank you, Grudnick, but it just isn't me. I'll keep the extra arm, though. It seems to be the only way to open doors around here."

Grudnick looked hard at me. Then she swung her arms up and removed contact lenses from two of her eyes.

"Your eyes!" I said. "They match. They're all orange."

Grudnick nodded. "I've been wearing lenses for years now," she said, "because I've been so ashamed."

"I think your eyes are beautiful," I said. "Of course, I only have two of them to see you with."

Grudnick laughed. "I guess we won't win the Miss Zyglot beauty pageant," she said.

"Frankly, I'm not going to bother entering," I said. And then I found myself humming the song "My Way."

"What's that?" Grudnick asked.

"It's my great-great-great-grandfather's favorite song," I told her. "He sings it all the time. His grandmother once knew someone who dated Frank Sinatra."

"Who's he?" Grudnick asked.

"He's a singer," I said. "They used to call him Old Blue Eyes. He only had two of them too."

"I guess that makes you Young Blue Eyes," Grudnick said.

"I guess so," I said. I rubbed my back against hers, which is how they hug on Zyglot. "You're the best, Grudnick. Or should I call you Young Orange Eyes?"

And we left the girl's room, laughing out loud, the two of us proud and strong, walking hand in hand together.

Nancy Springer

One sunny morning last summer, my best friend phoned me and said, "I'm painting my garage door and I need you to paint a dragon on it." My friend is an English teacher, and during summer vacation she goes a little crazy. "I don't know how to paint a dragon," she said. "Can you come over?" Well, of course. I was supposed to be working (writing), but who could resist? When I got there, she had completed a fantasy landscape of green hills and castle, and she was working on a rainbow and a smiley sun. Under the rainbow I painted a big purple and yellow flying dragon with a puff of flame coming out of its nostrils. It was fun.

My friend's garage door attracted so much attention that she started a small business of painting murals. But, get this—she felt so shy and insecure about calling herself an artist that she phoned a "real" artist and asked him for "permission" to paint.

I was thinking about that when I wrote this story.

A Blue Moon
in a White Sky

If we hadn't been so bored, none of this would have happened.

My father thinks boredom is good for kids. "Cultivate your own resources, Michael," he says whenever I ask to go to the mall or anything. What he means by that is that I should be spending my time making sculptures or something. My dad is chair of the College of Art & Design at the university, and our yard is full of his sculptures, which are pieces of twisted metal, kind of tortured-looking. They are painted black or primer orange or gray-green like canned peas or maybe dark red. Dad says they are postmodern nihilist abstraction, but I don't have a clue what that means. My dad tried to teach me to do art, but I can't even draw or paint, let alone sculpt. I mean, I used to try to draw something if he made me, like maybe a piece of driftwood he'd set up, or an old shoe—but whatever I drew was no good. He never said much, but the way he looked at my drawings, like he was opening the containers pushed to the back of the refrigerator, I knew they were no good. There is nothing artistic about me whatsoever. I mean, I would never say this, but I can't even see what's so great about Dad's sculptures.

So anyway, I don't try to do art anymore, but Dad wouldn't send me to summer camp. He wanted me to hang around the house and be bored. Shelley hung around my place a lot being bored too. Why her parents wouldn't send her to camp I don't know. At the time she was my new next-door neighbor in our development and I didn't know her very well yet.

"I wish we could go to the amusement park," I said, the day it all started. It was getting hot, and Parky Park had a killer new water ride.

Shelley perked up like a terrier. She is the same age as I am, thirteen, and she has a cute face and wears a lot of Winnie the Pooh clothes, but she is strong enough to beat me arm wrestling. "You got any money?" she demanded.

"No." That's another resource my dad wanted me to cultivate. He wanted me to earn my own spending money. Like how?

"You got a way to get there?"

"When we get to the end of the driveway we could just keep pedaling."

We were doing bike sprints. We would put our back tires against the garage door like it was a starting block and then we would peel out and pedal like mad to the end of the driveway. I have no idea why. We were so bored it seemed like a good idea at the time.

"Right. Sure," Shelley said. The amusement park was about thirty miles away. I guess she figured out we were not going to get there today. She swiped her hair back from her face with one hand. "I'm sweating. Let's go in. Look what we did to your garage door."

She said it in the exact same tone as "I'm sweating" and "Let's go in," like it didn't matter.

"Huh?" I looked, and I started to sweat, but not because I was hot. In fact I felt cold. "Oh. Oh, no." All over the garage door there were streaky black marks from our back bike tires.

You have to understand about my dad. In most ways he is a genuinely good guy, like he cooks excellent homemade pizza and he gets me into the university football games and he does the lettering on my school science projects for me, but he has what they call artistic temperament and he gets upset about things. And that garage door, he had just painted it. Pristine white.

"Oh," I groaned, and I guess Shelley could tell from my face that I was in real trouble.

"Hey, no problem," she said. "Where are your paper towels?"

But we couldn't get the garage door clean with paper towels and water, or spray cleaner, or even Comet cleanser. The black marks just stayed. The white paint started to smear and come off, though.

"Oh, *no*." I threw down my paper towel. "Shelley, I'm dead."

"No problem," she said like she had done too much baby-sitting in her life. "When's your dad get home?"

"Not till suppertime." And my mom was in Taiwan or someplace. She travels a lot for her job.

"Good, we got plenty of time," said Shelley with that same annoying patience. "Just paint over the messed-up places."

I had to admit that might work. We went into the garage through the side door to look for some white paint.

It's a two-car garage, but we don't put any cars in it. We park cars in the driveway, because the garage space is all taken up with my dad's shelves and workbenches and sheet metal and stuff. The main thing I know about art is that it is big and takes up a lot of space. What with all the sculptures my dad makes, he has a lot of power tools and a lot of junkyard salvage and a lot of paint.

"Wow," Shelley breathed. But she wasn't interested in Dad's latest sculpture, an eight-foot thing kind of like a metal snake with a bowling ball on top. She was staring at the ranks of paint cans.

"Here's the leftover white, I think." I hoped it was the same white he'd used on the garage door. I found a stirrer and some newspaper and a paintbrush and headed outside.

"Mars red," Shelley was whispering as she peered at the paint cans, "peacock blue, viridian, mustard yellow. . . ." I didn't hear the rest. Outside, I spread some newspaper, levered the white paint open, stirred it, and started stroking it over the smudges and black marks.

"Oh, CRUD!"

It didn't cover the black marks. They showed right through.

Besides, it looked dumb. Even when it was dry, it was still going to look dumb, my stupid brushstrokes on top of Dad's nice clean paint job.

I was dead.

I gave up. I folded and sat on the driveway where I was, just staring at the mess I'd made.

Shelley walked around the corner of the garage, looked at me, looked at the blobs of white paint I'd put on the garage door, looked at me again, and walked back the way she'd come.

I just sat there.

I heard Shelley come back. I didn't look at her.

"Mike," she said, "listen, it can't get any worse, right?"

The perky-terrier tone in her voice should have warned me, but my brain was too fried to think. "Right," I droned.

"Okay. So look here." She knelt down beside me, and when I looked over at her, she was painting a bright green swipe of paint on top of a black tire mark.

I yelped, "What? No! Don't!"

But she'd already switched brushes and was dipping into the Mars red. Three flicks of her wrist, and there was a big red tulip painted on my dad's garage door.

The green swipe was the stem. She added leaves. "There," she said, getting up and standing back to admire her work. "*That* covers the black mark."

I stared at her tulip. I don't know quite how to explain this, but her tulip was so bad it was good. It was so bright. So brave against the big white door. I liked it.

I knew if I ran and got turpentine and rags right away I could probably wipe it off.

I knew I wasn't going to.

"Gimme the white," Shelley said. "I want to mix some pink."

I think it was the idea of pink that did it. My dad just absolutely hates the color pink. And I kind of like it. There was a snapping feeling inside my head, like something either clicked together or broke loose, and all of a sudden I was calm and happy.

"Okay." I passed her the white paint, took the green and slashed a nice fat flower stem into place over another bike tire mark.

"My father is going to have a heart attack," I told Shelley the last minute before I stopped worrying about my father.

"Why should he? He wants you to do art, doesn't he?"

Shelley painted pink tulips. I painted red tulips and orange tulips. The orange really vibrated next to the pink. I painted yellow daffodils. Shelley filled in between the tulips with big blobby pink and blue hyacinths like cotton candy towers. "This is fun," I said. "You mix good colors." She mixed lavender and painted lavender hyacinths next. I painted blue daisies. I never had so much fun with paint. We didn't stop when we got all the bike tire marks covered. I stood up and put a big yellow sun up near the top of the garage door. Then I put a big peacock blue crescent moon with a spiky pink star in its arms.

Shelley was laughing at me. "Is it daytime up there, or night, or what?"

"I don't care. I'm going to paint anything I can think of that goes in a sky."

I painted more stars, all colors, and a red-and-white-striped hot-air balloon. I painted a purple and yellow dragon flying by. I painted a yellow Saturn with an orange ring, and some more planets. I painted cardinals and bluebirds flying around. I painted a flying saucer with a green alien peeking out the top of it. Hunkered down by my feet, Shelley painted grass around all the flowers. We didn't stop for lunch; we didn't even notice it was lunchtime or that we were sweating in the hot sun. We just kept going. I painted a biplane and a blimp. I painted a comet with a long tail. My yellow sun was dry now so I put a face on him, orange happy eyes and a big orange smile.

Shelley was putting a range of purple mountains behind the

flowers. She looked up at me and grinned. "If that's a sky," she said, "it should be blue."

She was right. So she mixed a sky blue and I started filling it in around my stars and stuff. Duh, should have done the background first. But it didn't matter. Shelley was filling in blue and yellow and green hills behind the flowers the same way. She left funky white outlines around the flowers and flower stems. It was all wrong but I liked the way it looked. I painted blue sky and I left funky white outlines around my planets and stars and aircraft too. And I left white places for clouds. It was hard for me to reach to the top of the garage door, and I didn't feel like going inside for a step stool, so I left that mostly white like it was a bunch of clouds. I even left a white place shaped like a bird, a white dove. Shelley started a big rainbow behind her mountains and arched it up into my sky, red, orange, yellow, green, blue, purple.

We covered that whole garage door with our picture. We painted all day long, and I never even noticed it was getting late, I was having so much fun, just painting the bright, smooth colors, not caring what anybody else might think. I was just putting some light gray on the underside of the white spaces I'd left to make them seem more like clouds when Dad drove in.

I couldn't see his face through the windshield, and I just stood there with my brush dripping. All of a sudden I didn't feel like I could paint anymore.

Then he got out of the car, and I did see his face, and I felt worse.

He didn't yell. He never yelled. I could have yelled back if he would just yell, but in our family we did not yell. "*What* is going on here?" Dad not-yelled between tight lips.

I couldn't answer, but Shelley, who was posing a yellow butterfly on top of one of her pink hyacinths, turned around and said to him, "Oh, hi, Professor." Everybody called him Professor.

"Michelle," he told her, "you had better go home."

"If it's the splatters on the driveway," she said like she was baby-sitting him now, "we can paint some black over them."

I looked down. I hadn't even noticed the newspapers had blown around and we'd dripped paint all over the driveway. I was sweating cold again.

"Michael, come here," Dad said. *"Michelle,* go home. *Now."*

I did what he said. Shelley gave me a worried look, laid down her paintbrush, and left.

I stood in the driveway not looking at Dad while he not-yelled at me. "Michael, *what* were you *thinking* of? Do you think this is responsible behavior? Who gave you permission. . ." And so on and so forth. I won't bore you with the whole lecture. It was what you might expect: I should have asked; Shelley might have helped, but I was to blame; if I couldn't set limits, then Shelley couldn't visit anymore; I had no business in his workshop or using his paints; did I have any idea how much paint cost; what a waste, now the whole garage door needed to be repainted; et cetera et cetera. I didn't try to explain about the bike tire marks or anything. It was no use. I didn't say a word. I just stood there and looked at the picture I had spent all day painting on the garage door, and now that Dad was home all I could see was all the things that were wrong with it. The way Shelley's rainbow was lopsided—it kind of veered to go between my hot-air balloon and my flying saucer. The way all the lines bumped and squiggled where there were joints and moldings in the garage door. The tulips looked stumpy. My flying dragon looked like a flying purple cow. My dove looked like an albino crow. It was no wonder Dad acted like Shelley and I had smeared the garage door with road kill.

Actually, he probably would have liked that better. It would have been a nihilist statement or something.

Actually . . . my brain started working a little bit, and I started to wonder. You know how sometimes parents get mad but the reasons they give you aren't the real reasons?

"I have a good mind to make you clean that trash off of there right now," Dad yelled. Dad was actually yelling? Whoa. "If we had enough turpentine I would. But it's going to take gallons of turp to get that garbage off of there."

Trash? Garbage?

"So now we've got to go for turpentine and white paint," he grumped, "first thing after supper. And you're paying for it. And you're paying for the paint you used today. And tomorrow and the next day and as long as it takes you're removing that so-called artwork. . . ."

I noticed that passing cars were slowing down so people could have a look. Just like they looked at Dad's sculptures. I could tell they were slowing down by the sounds of their engines as they paused at the bottom of the driveway. Some people almost stopped.

". . . and you're repainting the garage door the way it belongs. Starting six o'clock tomorrow morning. Now clean up this mess. And make sure you get all the paint can lids on *tight*." He stomped inside.

I knew he meant what he said about taking the painting off the garage door. Dad hardly ever told me what to do, but when he did, that was it. No use trying to change his mind.

After I hammered the lids back on the paint cans and cleaned the brushes and put everything back in the garage, I stood looking at the picture on the garage door some more to remind myself how crooked the rainbow was and everything.

It didn't work. I felt like Dad had told me to kill something.

Dad called me for supper and I went inside but I didn't eat.

Dad is a really good cook, and he had made three-cheese lasagna, which he knows I like, and I hadn't had anything to eat all day, but I just wasn't hungry. I sat at the table and watched my dad eat. He didn't look at me. I didn't look at him. I watched the fork move from his plate to his mouth and back again.

Somebody knocked on the door. I jumped to get it in case it was Shelley.

"Probably one of the neighbors complaining," Dad muttered as he heaved himself up from the table.

I got to the door first. Like Dad said, it was one of the neighbors—the neighbor lady from across the street. But she wasn't complaining.

"Mike!" she declared the minute I opened the door. "Your garage door is *beautiful*. I watched all day and it just kept getting more and more beautiful."

Something moved in the night behind the neighbor lady. It was Shelley and her dad. Right then I knew Shelley was going to be a best friend. She knew I was in trouble, so there she was. Bringing her dad over to talk with my dad.

"Thank you," I said to the neighbor lady, loud, so that everybody would hear, including my father, standing in the doorway behind me. Especially my father. "I'm glad you like it. *I like it too.*"

I did. I loved it. I didn't care how much stuff was wrong with it.

Shelley and her father were standing back, waiting their turn. Shelley looked very serious.

"Could you and your friend do one like it on my garage door for me? I'll pay you." The neighbor lady was so excited she just kept burbling along. "You know, garage doors are really ugly things. Big and ugly. And now yours looks so happy. I want mine to look just like yours. Except I want trees. And some deer and rabbits, and maybe a raccoon. Raccoons are my favorite animals. Can you do that?"

"Sure," I said, because I was just as qualified to paint trees and deer and rabbits as I was to paint the flying saucer and stuff on my garage door. "I think we can. Shelley?"

Shelley was starting to smile. "Sure."

"We can't start right away, though," I told the neighbor lady. "I've got to spend tomorrow and the next day et cetera scrubbing the picture off our garage door and repainting it white."

She stood there with her mouth open. Now she was looking at my father. "You—you don't like it??"

My father didn't answer. Shelley's father stepped forward. "That's what Shelley thought," he said to my father in a quiet, no-problem way. "She thought you might want it put back the way it was. She feels partly responsible. So I wanted to tell you, I got plenty of turpentine and white house paint the kids can use. Shelley will help Mike fix things up."

"But—but it's *beautiful!*" the neighbor lady not-quite-yelled at my father. "You should be *proud!*"

"Don't worry," I told her. "We'll make yours even better. I'll call you." I gave her a big smile, even though I didn't feel like smiling. Painting her garage door might be fun, but nothing would ever be quite the same as tulips and stars and a hot-air balloon and a blue moon in a white sky.

"I'll pay you kids fifty dollars each," she said, "plus the cost of the paint." She gave my father a killer look, turned, and stomped back toward her house.

"Thank you," my father said to Shelley and her father, and I don't think he meant to sound like he just wanted them to go away, but he did. He tugged me inside and closed the door.

He didn't say anything to me. There was an expression on his face I couldn't quite figure out because I'd never seen it there before.

The phone rang. I answered it.

"Is this the house with the mural on the garage door?" a man asked.

"Yes."

"You mind telling me who painted it? I want to see if they can paint me one."

"Um, I'm the painter." I pretended not to notice that Dad was listening in. "Me and my friend, I mean. What do you think you'd like in your mural?"

He wanted a farm scene with cows and stuff. I started taking notes. I told him fifty dollars apiece for Shelley and me. When I got done talking with him and looked up, Dad was gone.

That was okay with me. I called Shelley and told her we had another job.

"Hey," she said, "this is pretty amazing. What's your dad think?"

"I don't know."

"Is he still mad? I can't believe he's so mad. My dad says if we'd done it to his garage door, he might have yelled at us some, but then again, look at the Sistine Chapel. He's not flipped out about it. What's the matter with your dad?"

I thought about the weird expression I'd seen on my dad's face. "I don't think he's still mad, exactly. He's just . . ." I didn't know. "He's just not talking to me."

"Well, *you* talk to *him*, Mike, will you?"

Shelley gave good advice. I hung up the phone and I thought about painting the picture on the garage door and how good it felt and I thought about my dad and then I went looking for him.

He was in his garage workshop. He has an old armchair in there and he was sitting in it, just sitting and staring at his half-finished metal sculpture.

I checked out his face again. That look was still there, and all of a sudden I understood it. He was sulking.

Sulking. My *father*. Isn't it illegal for parents to sulk?

I sat down on his workbench stool facing him. I said, "Me'n Shelley got another job."

"Shelley and I."

"No, *me*. Not you." I was trying to joke around, pretending not to understand that he was correcting my grammar, but he gave me a glare fit to frost my socks. I sighed and said, "What's this really about, anyway?"

He gave me the same look, but I didn't shut up. I had made up my mind not to shut up, because the painting on the garage door was important. To me. And somehow that made me strong and calm. I said, "It's not about me not asking permission. You don't make me ask permission for anything else I decide to do; like, if I go bungee jumping or join the Navy, just leave a note. And it's not about me using your paints. You're always trying to get me to do art, you always told me to use your stuff, you never told me not to."

Now he looked kind of stunned. I had never talked to him like this before.

I wasn't trying to get him to change his mind about the garage door, either. I knew he never changed his mind once he told me to do something. I just wanted him to understand.

I asked him again, "So what's it really about?"

He said, sarcastic, "What do *you* think it's about?"

"I think it's because you don't like the painting."

I was right, I knew I was right, I saw it in his eyes. But he tried to cover up by acting like a professor. "Well, it *is* quite representational," he said like he was talking to a really dense student, "and rather primitivistic. I—"

When he talks like that I get annoyed. I interrupted. "What makes your stuff better? Your sculptures? Is it because people like them more?"

"Well, no. They don't, evidently. It's just—"

"Is there some sort of Ten Commandments of Art that says your stuff is better?"

"Well, yes, sort of. It's—"

I said, real hard, "So you only approve of me if I do the kind of art you like, right?"

He gawked at me. He opened his mouth and shut it again.

I got up and left. I made a point of not slamming the door.

I went to bed, but I couldn't sleep. I guess I dozed a little. But it was not hard for me to get up early like Dad had said, because I was lying there wide awake.

So at six in the morning I walked out the front door to get started. To kill tulips, rainbow, purple mountains, stars and comets and sun and dove, flying saucer, blue moon, red-and-white-striped hot-air balloon, everything.

I would have done it, too. Except Dad was there ahead of me.

He was painting a gold banner across the top of the garage door. He is taller than I am, so he could reach higher.

And, get this, he was surprised to see me. "Mike, what are you doing up so early?"

I didn't want to say because he'd told me to. I said, "I couldn't sleep." I stood there staring. Maybe it was just too early in the morning, but I couldn't understand what was going on.

Dad looked at me, laid down his paintbrush, came over to me and hugged me. "Forget everything I said," he told me, gruff. "Go back to bed."

All of a sudden I felt so much better that I couldn't say a word for a minute. I leaned against him. He had really changed his mind? But—but why? What was going on?

"I don't get it." My voice came out husky. I stepped back to look at him.

He flushed and looked down at his hands. "You made me think, that's all. I never knew I was such a snob. But I am." He glanced at the garage door, at the funky tulips and Mr. Happy Sun and everything, and he almost smiled. "You want to know the first thing that went through my mind when I saw this? I was afraid people might look at it and think that *I* painted it."

"Oh, good grief." Now I understood, and I couldn't help it, I had to laugh. Dad looked mortified, but then he grinned, and then he started laughing too. We both laughed like idiots.

"So what goes on the banner?" I asked him when we were mostly done laughing.

"Well, that's up to you. I thought maybe 'MURALS BY MIKE AND MICHELLE.' Since you two kids seem to be going into the garage-door mural business."

I told him, "Do it the other way around. 'MURALS BY MICHELLE AND MIKE.' "

"Sounds like a plan to me." He started painting the banner again. After he was done painting it he would do the lettering. Red lettering, I decided. I thought about going back to bed but I felt too good. I sat on the driveway and took it all in. The picture, the flying dragon, and blue crescent moon, and blimp, and everything—under that golden banner it all looked so bright. And right. And big. Like real art.

"After you and Michelle do another couple of murals," Dad called to me, "you should start holding out for a hundred dollars apiece."

Like real artists. Dad always said artists should hold out for better pay. I smiled. Then a thought flew in like a butterfly lighting on my head.

"Hey, Dad," I called, "I guess I cultivated me a resource!"

"For once in a blue moon, yes, you did."

So that's how "MURALS BY MICHELLE AND MIKE" got started.

And like I said, none of it would have happened if we weren't so bored. Which was a good thing. All the rest of that summer, Shelley and I had plenty of money to go to Parky Park whenever we wanted—only we never did. We were too busy painting great stuff on people's garage doors, which was more fun anyway. Red, orange, yellow, green, blue, purple fun.

Virginia Euwer Wolff

More than a decade ago I taught in a medium-size public high school. The school was designed so that teachers had "cubes" instead of office areas. One morning a sophomore girl came to me on the verge of tears. Let's say her name was Darlene. (It wasn't.) "Ms. Wolff, I left a dozen roses in your cube," she said, trying to stay in control of some terrible internal storm.

I almost said thank you.

"They're from Danny." (Not his real name, either.) She was breathless.

I almost smiled.

"I don't want them. . . ." Her voice was poignant, pained, and clear. She began to sob. I put my arms around her and waited.

"I broke up with him. He knows it— He won't accept it— He's just trying to manipulate me—"

What astonished me then, and has stayed with me ever since, was the wisdom of a fifteen-year-old girl who knew that flowers were the boy's method of trying to bend her will. To get her to stop honoring her own instincts and instead yield to his power.

"Dozens of Roses: A Story for Voices" is fiction. It's intended to be read aloud, and it's not really about Darlene. But without her, I doubt that I would ever have found my way to it. I have so often thought of that very young girl who had the strength to resist a dozen red roses. This story is a tribute to her.

Dozens of Roses: A Story for Voices

Voices: Lucy
       Chuck
       Chorus
       The Rememberer

Chorus: They are bloodred, floating on long stems, stiffened with invisible wire so they stand up straight among maiden-hair ferns, and there are a dozen of them.

Lucy: I don't want them.

Chorus: But they came for you! A dozen red roses! Delivered by a florist's messenger! Right to the school office! An announcement came over the air, through the walls, into all the hallways, asking for you to come to the office!

Lucy: I don't want them. Please don't make me take them.

The Rememberer: I used to know her when we were little. She was full of energy then. We had picnics and we played jump rope. She had pep.

Chorus: Who sent them to you?

Lucy: Please don't make me say.

Chorus: You can't ignore flowers. There they are, standing up straight in a vase full of water, right in front of the secretary's desk. It's really a sight to see: the dull old school office, with the tan walls and the tan filing cabinets and bad lighting— And those dozen romantic, red roses.

Chuck: She'll know how I feel about her when she sees the roses.

Lucy: I can't go get them.

Chorus: That's ridiculous. Of course you can go get them. Who would turn down such a gift?

Lucy: You don't understand.

Chorus: Oh—you mean your sprained ankle? They must be get-well roses.

Lucy: I don't care what kind of roses they are.

The Rememberer: Something has taken the fire out of her. She isn't the same.

Chorus: Take a friend with you. To help carry them while you limp along. Read the card and tell us who sent them.

Chuck: She'll love them. That's a lot of money I spent.

Chorus: Whoever he is, he must adore you.

Lucy: I won't look at them. I won't go to the office. I won't read the card.

Chuck: She'll forget she was mad.

Chorus: You're a lucky girl.

Lucy: My ankle hurts.

Chorus: People who feel sorry for themselves aren't any fun at all.

Chuck: She fell.

Lucy: I can't leave my math class.

Chuck: She fell right over the end of the chair.

Lucy: Please, somebody, take the roses home with you.

Chorus: You must be crazy.

Chuck: She had her weight distributed the wrong way. I barely touched her.

Chorus: She must be very stubborn.

Chuck: She looked at him. I saw her look at him. Making plans to meet him behind my back.

Lucy: I need to do my math.

The Rememberer: Maybe it was that cut on her forehead last fall. Maybe it did something to her brain. Maybe the emergency room was a shock to her system.

Chorus: She's so ungrateful.

Lucy: Please don't make me talk about it.

Chuck: She'll know when she gets the roses. How much I feel for her.

Lucy: I want to stay in class, where I can breathe.

Chuck: I need her. She'll know when she gets the roses.

The Rememberer: That *was* it. When she had to go to the hospital that time. With the cut on her forehead. She's been different ever since.

Lucy: Can math class please go on forever?

Chorus: There's a time to be moody and a time to snap out of it. She should snap out of it.

Chuck: I can't live without her. She'll know when she gets the roses.

The Rememberer: She got a dozen roses that other time, too.

Suzanne Fisher Staples

At the age of ten or so I was deeply embarrassed by my mother. She was overweight, outspoken, religious, strict, and determined to be physically comfortable at the expense of fashion. Rather than flats or loafers or even high heels, she wore dark brown oxfords and folded-down white socks. She wore frumpy housedresses that hitched up in the back. She wore her hair in a mannish, slicked-back style. She sneezed so loudly people ducked, then turned to stare at her. And worst of all, she always said exactly what was on her mind.

Then one day my grandmother fell gravely ill in Philadelphia. My mother, who I hardly ever saw cry, packed a "grip," tears streaming down her face. We all went along when my father drove her to the airport. I sat behind her in the car, watching as she tried to attach a straw pillbox hat to her impossibly short hair with a hat pin and straighten the collar on her going-to-church coat. I was overcome with a feeling of love for her and shame at myself for the embarrassment I felt over her. In that moment, what mattered most was that she was loving, loyal, honest, and uncommonly decent and kind.

Unfortunately the effects of this epiphany did not last. As I grew into my teens, more embarrassments heaped on earlier ones, compounding my guilt as I failed to conquer my concern over appearances, and my mother became ever more retrenched in her pursuit of comfort and sensibility.

I had several friends whose mothers I greatly admired. One mother was intellectual, sophisticated, chic, and eccentric in a Bohemian way. My secret wish was that I could claim my friend's mother as my own. Many years later, when my friend and I were out of college, I was astonished to learn that she had coveted *my* mother—she longed for someone who would bake cookies to put on the counter after school, sit her down on a stool to detangle her hair, wash her back in the tub, and who wouldn't allow her to stay out past dark, no matter what the other mothers did. I learned later that what I had perceived as exotic eccentricity in her mother was in fact a profound suffering due to alcohol and emotional instability.

The memory of my mother that night sticks in my mind as an early inkling of the importance of family and loyalty and having people who care about you no matter what you wear or how you think or what you believe in. And, almost as important, it was the first time I realized that appearances are mainly puny things.

Klesmer

When I remember my mother I think of her playing the violin, a fast-paced haunting tune. The soul pours out of her dark cinnamon eyes as she stares across the strings, down at her fingers lying lightly over the bow.

And she sings with a voice like quicksilver, agile and bright and clear. It's a strange sort of music, half spoken, half hummed, which she accompanies by plucking the strings of her violin like a harp. On the high notes her voice does a kind of flip, turning over on itself in a way that takes my breath away.

Her name was Klesmer, and she's been dead for a year. The word means a kind of violin made by the wandering people of the Carpathian Mountains, which, though she'd never been there, my mother called home. My memory is of a tall woman with long, wavy black hair, swirling red skirts, long green beads that I'd teethed on as an infant, and rows of silver bracelets that slid up and down her slender arms.

They said she was crazy as a loon, and that was why I couldn't stay with her any longer.

Until she left my father six years ago, what people said about Klesmer was that she was so charming, so eccentric, so much fun. My mother was funny and imaginative to an extreme, with a poet's heart that was too large for her own good.

She left home with all of her belongings spilling out of a wicker basket. On top was the cage that held her dearest possession, Tatin, our African gray parrot.

"I'm a dead duck," Tatin would say, his voice a miserable croak. He'd hop down to the floor of his cage and lie on his back, his feet thrusting into the air. A few seconds later he'd right himself and pull himself back up to his perch. "I'm a dead duck," he'd say again. Tatin always hated to leave the house.

I'm not sure what happened to Klesmer beginning at about the time she left us. Did she begin to disintegrate? Did my father's anger force her over the edge? Or perhaps I began to see her differently because of the awful things he'd said about her.

I may never know whether she was really crazy. In the good times I found her slightly embarrassing, perhaps, but the wheels were definitely on the rails.

She'd come to get me at school, telling the principal's office there was a family emergency. Then she'd take me out for a drive along Tampa Bay and feed me hot dogs and ice cream. We'd look out over the water at a necklace of lights, with Tatin in the back seat screeching that he was a dead duck.

Later I grew ashamed of Klesmer, even a little frightened by her bizarre behavior. But it was as if she'd cast a spell over me, and I couldn't resist her. Even now I long for her.

Klesmer moved from our apartment in Tampa to St. Petersburg. I don't know where she stayed at first. My father said she slept on the street and ate from garbage cans like a bum. I asked her, but she wouldn't say. She came back to visit me and have terrible fights with my father that ended with him slamming the door on both of us, sending us off with a curse.

Then Klesmer ran into a streak of luck, a "cosmic intervention," she called it, and I suppose that meant she somehow came into a little money.

With it she set up shop in a tiny cottage between two motels on the beach in St. Petersburg, where she told fortunes. Incense burned from pots on the floor. She kept the blinds drawn, so the light was filtered, smoky, and refracted by strings of red and yellow plastic beads she hung over the blinds.

Klesmer came to get me at 7:30 on a Saturday morning. She and my father had their last horrible argument. My father's curses cracked and ended in splintered high pitches. He kicked his foot through the front door of the apartment. They left it up to me to decide who I wanted to live with.

My father didn't make much of a case. He paced back and forth in the bedroom of the apartment in a T-shirt, his hands slipped into the back pockets of his jeans.

"I know you don't like it here," he said, "but I can't afford better. And you know I travel a lot." He shook his head as if he knew it was a no-go. "I'll hate losing you," he added, almost as if he'd just thought of it.

I felt sorry for him, and realized I hardly knew him at all. Compared to Klesmer he was about as interesting to me as a white sheet. And he was right: I hated it there.

The apartment was surrounded by asphalt that heated to stovetop temperatures. Summers it was littered with the parched corpses of grasshoppers and frogs and worms that'd wandered too far from the grass. There wasn't even a swimming pool.

I was to spend that weekend with Klesmer. When we got to

the cottage, we sat in the living room and sipped lemonade. It was a muggy late summer day. The salt- and mud-scented Gulf breeze rattled the plastic beads at the windows and the grass out front hissed and whispered. My mother set our glasses down and put her arms around me. She pulled me over beside her on the uncomfortable, shawl-draped couch.

"Liara, honey," she whispered against my hair. "You ease my soul. You ease my soul, and I need you." Her voice sounded desperate, and that settled it.

My father raged out of the apartment when we come back for my stuff. He slammed the door and screeched his rusted blue Honda out of the driveway.

"Ma," I said. "Was Dad crying?" I'd never seen such a thing and thought since I felt a bit like crying myself I might've imagined it.

"Don't be silly," she said. "He has no tears."

We loaded everything I owned into the back of Klesmer's latest acquisition, a beat-up yellow Olds. I didn't have much: a box of puzzles, an old Barbie doll who had permanently bad hair, three dresses that were too short for me, my good shoes, two pairs of lace-trimmed baby doll pajamas—one pink and one blue—a pair of worn purple jellies, a bag of colored socks, and a mismatched assortment of T-shirts and shorts. Oh, and a bathing suit and a soccer ball.

I've never forgiven my father for not coming back to say good-bye to me, and I began to be suspicious about all the things he'd said about Klesmer that made me ashamed of her and afraid of what she might do next. And he never came to visit me after I moved to the cottage. So much for him.

Klesmer enrolled me in a school that was just a three-block walk from the cottage. Still, she came to get me every after-noon in the Olds, which had big fins and made me think of castles and dragons. I wanted to walk with the other kids. I got so I dreaded seeing her in the Olds, smoke curling out the window from a cigarette held gracefully between her long brown fingers.

The other moms went to step aerobics together and looked like models. There wasn't one of them who didn't have long tanned legs coming out of their neon-colored jogging shorts with matching bicycle tights underneath. And they wore their blond hair cut in cunning little bobs.

By comparison with the other moms everything about Klesmer seemed exaggerated, as if she'd just stepped out of a cheap fifties movie. Her hair was never arranged—it always seemed out of control and out of proportion to her desperate, crimson-mouthed face.

The day I met Moira Quinn she squinted up at me and said, "Where'd you come from?" Moira had reddish-blond thick wavy hair and creamy skin. Her eyes were the color of Tampa Bay on a brilliant day. She was small and athletic-looking. Looking down at her I felt positively gawky—too tall, too skinny, big-footed and plain.

She explained she didn't mean to be unkind.

"You're just so exotic," Moira said. "I thought maybe you were an exchange student." It was a pretty good recovery, and I liked her immediately.

Moira's passion was poetry, and I so wanted Moira to think well of me I got off to a good start in my academic life. Moira was an intellectual snob. To my amazement I aped her in English class with the greatest of ease. I don't think she expected me to keep up with her, but I remember the day she began to respect me.

"Why do you suppose," Mr. Gregory asked the class, "that Coleridge speaks of 'this lime tree bower' as 'my prison'?" My hand flew up even before Moira's. "Liara?" said Mr. Gregory, flicking the end of his pencil in my direction.

"He's a prisoner of loneliness because his friends have left him, and he's feeling lost," I replied eagerly. Out of the corner of my eye I saw Moira's head turn sharply toward me. She was surprised how well I'd understood the poem.

That day I joined Moira in the lofty if lonely sphere of truly gifted students. The other kids deferred to us in class. We were so arrogant! We didn't need them. If they made fun of us or talked about us behind our backs we were too absorbed in each other and our poetry to know.

I longed for Klesmer to behave like Mrs. Quinn. Moira's mother would pick us up from school and take us to their pink stucco house with high arching windows in a gated subdivision out along the Bay. The Quinns' pool sat amid a lush garden of birds-of-paradise and ferns and overhanging orchids that was guarded all around by a thick wall of swaying bamboo, all of which was coccooned in brown screen. Moira and I would splash around in the turquoise water while Mr. Quinn cooked steaks on the grill.

I'd lie on my back just beneath the surface in the deep end of the white-tiled pool, my head tilted back, gazing up at the silver skin the water laid over the sky. I thought it was perhaps the most serene place on earth. I even loved the sting of chlorine in my nose and eyes.

I lived with the guilty knowledge that if I'd had a choice of mothers Klesmer would have been gone in a heartbeat in favor of Mrs. Quinn. Moira's mother stayed home afternoons baking oatmeal raisin cookies so we'd have something to eat after school. Klesmer sat in a darkened room communing with the spirits of her ancestors who dwelt beside a rock-strewn goat track high in the Carpathian Mountains.

I invited Moira home once, and then only because she insisted.

The front door was locked. Moira was impressed that I had a key. Her mother was always home when Moira got there, and the Quinns' door was never locked.

"Ma!" I called. "Are you home, Klesmer?" (My mother liked me to call her by her first name.) At first there was no reply. Something bumped in the next room.

"Oh! Ahh-hh! Oh!" came from behind the wall.

"Ma!" I shouted too loudly. I was mortified. "It's me. And Moira. What are you *do*ing?!" A few moments later Klesmer emerged from the next room looking wild as a condor. Her hair was more disheveled than ever and her eyes were red-rimmed and spooked.

"Ma!" I shouted. "What were you doing in there?" She didn't answer. "Oh," I moaned, turning toward Moira, "of all the days to bring you home with me!" Moira stared wide-eyed, taking in Klesmer, the painted camel-skin lamp, the beaded curtains, the incense smoking in pots of sand at the base-boards, the bright sunlight filtered obscurely through the red plastic beads.

"Christabel!" Moira murmured. She was awestruck by my mother. From that time on she always asked about Klesmer, but I would never bring her home with me again, though she asked me to about every week.

Then Klesmer began to insist I stay home from school.

"It's time you learned the important things," she'd say.

"I *am* learning the important things," I shouted back at her. "Math. English. Science. Ma, I can't function in the world if I don't know this stuff."

Klesmer's idea of the important things was learning how to make stinking brews that she said cured warts and other things I didn't feel the need of curing. And cultivating exotic mush-rooms that we sold at the county fair. And learning to recite refrains in the obscure Carpathian dialect she called her mother tongue. The refrains, she said, were to result in spells cast over the enemies of her clients.

Most of her clients were migrant workers. I felt like telling them they should spend their money more wisely. When one of these unfortunates was willing, Klesmer had me sit beside her at the India-cotton-draped table as she traced the heart and head and health lines in an outstretched palm. She'd turn off all the lights and urge me to see the aura shooting out around the head and shoulders of someone who needed to buy new shoes, needed a haircut or a new dress. Some of them left their babies alone out in the front hall while they listened, entranced, to Klesmer.

Before long a social services worker came to see us. Klesmer said we were home-schooling.

"I'd like to see your lesson plans, please," said Mrs. Thomas, the social worker. She was a heavy-set, pleasant-looking woman. She wore a denim dress with a red bandana tied at the throat. "I'll come back Wednesday," she said with a skeptical look when Klesmer said she hadn't finished that week's plan yet.

Biding her time, Klesmer sent me back to school. She forbid me to see Moira, who my mother said had a bad influence on me.

I was too ashamed to tell Moira, so I simply avoided her. She was hurt at first. She'd come up behind me in the hall and say, "Liara, what did I do? You've got to talk to me!" But I'd just speed away from her.

In the meantime Klesmer's business dropped off and we moved to an abandoned school bus that sat in a clearing just off the long dirt road that followed the river out of town. It was hot and damp and dusty and I was miserable. Klesmer called our new home Troll Hollow. She seemed happy and I wondered if it was just me. Maybe we'll be all right, I thought.

Klesmer came to get me at school on a rainy March day. She walked right into eighth grade English without knocking. Her dress was wet and clung translucently to her legs. Her hair was pinned up, but had half fallen down with slick fronds plastered to her face and neck. She clutched a jade green shawl about her wide shoulders.

Mr. Gregory looked up in astonishment at the wild-eyed apparition that had burst through the doorway of his classroom.

"Can I help you?" he asked.

"I've come for Liara," she said. Her eyes slid around the room, passing over me twice. I had hunched down in my seat without realizing it. "What have you done with her?"

"Who are you?" Mr. Gregory asked.

"I'm her mother," said Klesmer.

"Liara?" said Mr. Gregory. Twenty-two pairs of eyes turned on me in amazement and disapproval, as if my mother had just announced that I was a leper. The blood roared in my ears. My face felt hot and flushed. A knot of nerves leapt and quivered in a spot somewhere between my shoulder blades.

Klesmer ran up and down the classroom aisles looking for me, her soggy skirts swirling out around her as she turned to go down the next row of seats.

I stood. I wanted to get out of there as quickly as possible. I leaned over to close my notebook and gather the books into my backpack.

"Liara, honey," Klesmer said, spotting me. She climbed through a row of seats, knocking David Brandt sideways in his chair. "Liara," she said again, her voice breathless and frightened. "Come on. You won't be needing your books. Come on."

She circled my wrist in her slender brown fingers and pulled on me desperately. "Let's get out of here!"

"What are you doing?" I asked in the hallway, out of earshot of my classmates. I tried to stop her, force her to face me and explain, but she hauled on my arm all the way to her car, which smelled of mildew.

"Where are we going?" I asked. Tatin was in the back seat.

"Home," she said. I thought she was afraid my father was looking for us, and that he might follow us, and—I don't know what-all she imagined he'd do.

"I'm a dead duck," Tatin screeched and fell to the floor of his cage.

The day the social services woman came for me it also stormed. The rain beat in waves over the roof of the school bus. The smell of ozone crackled in the air. Next to the over-turned crate we used for a step an orange hibiscus bloomed with an aching beauty like neon against the soggy gray morning.

Tatin whistled a bar of one of my mother's haunting melodies. Then, "I'll be pummeled!" he shouted, jumping down from his perch to cock his head at the clatter of the storm.

Klesmer sat at the windshield and watched the drops raise dust in the unpaved road that led from Tampa. Out back in the swamp a gator bellowed. It was mating season and the bulls kept up a ruckus day and night.

A white sedan with government of Florida plates front and back lurched slowly down the road. Mrs. Thomas got out and made her way toward the open school bus door through the mud under a huge dripping black umbrella.

"Liara, get the basket," said Klesmer. She inclined her head over her shoulder toward a pile of old clothes in the back. Atop it sat a basket of what looked like my socks.

"What's in it?" I asked.

"Go," said Klesmer. I did.

"Fine day," Klesmer said out the door to Mrs. Thomas, who stood there under her umbrella looking uncomfortable. A strange prickle began to prance up and down my spine.

"You know why we've come," said Mrs. Thomas. She wore

the same denim dress and red bandana knotted jauntily at her throat. Klesmer smiled at her, and Mrs. Thomas motioned to a female police officer standing behind her under yet another streaming black umbrella. "May we come in?"

They came in and Mrs. Thomas took me into the back of the bus while the policewoman talked to my mother. The police officer was a heavyset black woman. She stood between us, and I couldn't see Klesmer as Mrs. Thomas talked.

"Liara, honey," she said, "I'm Miz Thomas. Remember me?" I nodded at her stupidly. Why was she talking to me like I was six years old?

"Don't call me 'honey,' " I said.

"You know," she said, sitting on the daybed across from me and leaning close to my face. "Your mama, she's a good person, but she's having problems right now. She needs help." The smell of face powder was suffocating.

"Ma!" I hollered.

"Don't worry," Klesmer said from the front of the bus. "Listen to what the lady tells you."

"While your mom is getting help," Mrs. Thomas went on, "we're going to have you stay with a nice family. You'll have plenty to eat, there are other kids and lots of toys. . . ."

"Ma!" I shouted. I was beginning to panic. "Ma! What's she talking about?"

"Don't worry," Klesmer said. She was pinning her hair up, talking around the hairpins she had pressed between her lips. "Don't worry, honey, you'll be fine."

I loved her desperately in that moment. I knew she was the only family I'd ever had, ever would have, crazy or not. I remembered the zany things we did to have fun: eating jelly beans on the ferris wheel, dancing together at the old dance hall downtown, collecting shells at the beach. So many things ran through my mind, but what I mainly remember is the aching love.

Occasionally I take down Klesmer's violin. Its wood shines darkly, the color of my mother's eyes. I don't know whether it's memory—I don't remember her teaching me—or perhaps I was born with the knowledge of the music in my fingers. I look across the strings at my fingers resting lightly over the bow, and play a fast-paced haunting melody, and half speak, half hum Klesmer's music.

Sharon Dennis Wyeth

I remember: I am in the back of a car. I am wearing my hair in pigtails. I feel very clean and dressed up and quiet. I am ten years old. My mother is in front on the passenger side. She is smiling at the lady who is driving us. She seems excited and her hair, which is long and wavy and black, looks very beautiful and she has on orange lipstick. I can only see the back of the woman who is the driver. She is a wide person. She is talking very politely. She looks at me for a moment in the rearview mirror. "Your child . . . ," she says to my mother, "she looks, well . . ." She sighs. "Your skin—are you part Indian?" Then my mother, who has browner skin than I, because I take after my father's family who is light-skinned, says to the lady in a quiet, firm voice: "I am not Indian. We are Negro." Suddenly the car pulls over. The lady who is driving gets out and starts to talk on the telephone. When she gets back into the driver's seat, she makes a turn onto the highway, heading back in the direction we'd just come from. "I'm sorry," she says to my mother, "the people who own the house don't want to be the first ones . . ."

"White" Real Estate

We already had a house. It was on Twenty-fifth Street. It wasn't the first house we'd owned or at least lived in. When my mother and father got back together for the last time, they moved into a house owned by my father's sister, my Aunt Julie. Aunt Julie had several houses and didn't live in Washington, D.C., so she thought she'd might as well rent this one to her brother. It was a big house on Second Street in N.W. It had an attic, a backyard, and a garage. My brothers and I played with kittens there. My mother and father also had to take in some boarders, because my father kept gambling away the money he made at what people said was a very good job. On my father's side of the family and in the small town in Virginia where he came from, he was kind of a celebrity; whenever I'd go to the country to visit my grandparents and they would introduce me as Creed, Jr.'s, little girl, I was met with admiring glances. "Looks just like him," they'd say. "Smart as a tack, Creed, Jr. He could go anywhere in this world. Got him a good government job. Got himself into the Air Force. Couldn't nobody do math like Creed, Jr." But there we were on Second Street taking in boarders. Not that my mother didn't work, too. She was also smart, rising in the ranks of government from typist to secretary to technical writer. She had wanted to be a musician and trained all her life for it. She never got the chance to see that dream transform; it simply vanished when she had me at the age of seventeen and then three boys. She interviewed the very best housekeepers to take care of us while she went to work. We had Mrs. Fisher, who wore uniforms, and Helen, who was eighteen years old and ate salt on her apples and sat out on the front stoop of the fancy house and picked her toes. Mr. and Mrs. Moon lived upstairs in what used to be my mother's and father's bedroom, after Daddy kept coming home drunk and out of cash week after week. Then one day, we were out of there. Mommy and my three brothers and I. Daddy had added insult to injury by starting to beat her again. I never knew what Mr. and Mrs. Moon thought. But after their last try at Second Street, my parents' marriage was gone for good. And so was the house and everything in it. I didn't know it at the time, but

Mommy was running for our lives. There was no time to pack up the china or the kittens.

So we stayed at Nana's and Granddaddy's tiny, neat row house in Southeast Washington. In those days, the Anacostia section which was recently called "forgotten" on the front page of the *New York Times,* was kind of like the country. Nana and Granddaddy's house was the next to the last on the block. Across the alley was an apartment development; the buildings were light orange brick, three-story affairs, each with a concrete walk leading to a longer, winding concrete walk that connected the buildings. After a brief stay at Nana and Granddaddy's, where we four kids slept sardine-style across one bed, the apartments across the alley are where Mommy and our little family ended up. As I mentioned, that area of D.C. was pretty rural at the time; beyond the apartment complex there were dense woods—an inviting wilderness just outside the window. That summer, my three brothers and I went to the real country—to stay with our other grandparents in Virginia. Daddy spent three days with us, the highlight of the trip. But nothing could match the excitement I experienced when we got back to D.C. and my mother announced that we had moved and drove us to the very first house we owned, which she'd purchased by herself—a semi-detached redbrick with white shutters on Twenty-fifth Street, S.E. There were only two bedrooms, but everyone had his/her own bed. I'll never forget the thrill of seeing the room I was to share with Mommy for the very first time. There were white frilly curtains in the window and fresh white chenille spreads with pompons on the twin beds. On the floor in between was a red, white, and blue woven rag rug that Nana had made for us. A whole corner of the room was reserved just for me. I recognized a small chest which held my clothes and a real desk which Mommy had found at the Salvation Army and Granddaddy had painted for me. I loved desks so much. I had never had one before. The first thing I did was sit down beneath it and go through the cardboard box which held my treasures—a stash of bubble gum comics I was collecting in order to send away for a "real pearl" necklace; the only two books I owned, *Black Beauty* and *Tom Sawyer* and a picture of my father in his Air Force uniform. For a long time that's the way I used the desk—rather than sitting at it, I sat underneath, creating a den for myself.

The house on Twenty-fifth Street was terrific from my point of view. There were even some old friends from the apartment complex whose mother had the same idea and had bought a house down the street. Soon my brothers and I were all set up with playmates. The house was within walking distance of a playing field that we referred to as a park. There was also a small shopping center and a bus stop right on our block. My mother took that bus to work every morning, after leaving us a hot breakfast on the stove, usually cream of wheat or oatmeal. My brothers and I played in our new backyard after school. We never ever got tired of climbing up the small slope that we thought of as a hill and rolling down into a pile of leaves. After the pile was scattered, my brother Milton would get the rake and build it up until it was high again. Up we'd trudge, then lie down in a row and roll down together, bumping into one another, giddy with laughter. Other nice things about the house were the staircase, great for sliding; and the basement, where we put the television. Soon after we'd moved in, Nana hired a truck to move over my mother's old piano. That pretty much took up the living room, along with the red convertible couch which my mother used to sleep on when we had the apartment and which we kids had now jumped the springs out of. The dining area had our old kitchenette set. For a housewarming gift, my mother's sister, my Aunt Carolyn, had given us some new plastic dishes. Nobody could have convinced me that we weren't elegant. Even when I began to take

piano lessons from Mrs. Proctor, who turned out to be the
mother of Joyce, my best friend in school, and noticed that
they had two couches with pink and white slipcovers and all
the springs and that Joyce had a room to herself with a shelf
full of books and a collection of brand-new-looking stuffed animals—even then, I would not have traded her house for ours
on Twenty-fifth Street. I never wanted to leave. That's why
when I heard my mother making her plans to go look at real
estate, I was angry and baffled.

"I don't want to move again," I told her one night. I was
crying into my pillow. "I don't want to leave my friends. We've
moved enough times."

I couldn't understand. What reason was there to run away
from Twenty-fifth Street? Daddy wasn't giving us any trouble.
In fact, aside from the times we ran into him in the country,
we never heard from him. It was only years later that I understood why: he was dodging the child support payments. My
mother must have been furious, but she never let us know
about it. Whenever my brothers or I brought up the subject of
our father, recounting some funny thing we'd done with him,
like eating hot peppers and playing a game we liked called
"Devil and the Pies," my mother would smile and listen. And
she never disturbed the picture of him I kept on our dresser.
When I tried to figure out the reason why Daddy never called
or visited, I felt a great ache inside. So I decided not to think
about it. Instead, I enjoyed the peace and quiet that came with
his absence and the joy on my mother's face as she joined us
in our backyard and raked leaves with us or cooked our Sunday dinners in the tiny kitchen.

But it seemed that the neighborhood I'd come to feel so at
home in was "dangerous," according to Mommy. There were
robberies and winos all over the place, she complained. There
were boys who would take notice of me that she definitely
didn't want me hanging around with. Then there were the

schools—I was a smart girl, she said, I was "gifted"; there were schools in other neighborhoods that would be much better for me and for my brothers. She wanted the best for us. She wanted a room for herself and she wanted one just for me; she wanted my brothers away from the boys who were always getting into trouble. Those were her reasons. I didn't believe her. She wanted to find a house in another area altogether. Even though I was only in fifth grade, I knew that it was a mistake. Twenty-fifth Street was where we belonged—a quick ride or a long walk from Nana's and Granddaddy's; my oldest friends were just down the street and up the hill in a fancier house, was my best friend, Joyce, and Mrs. Proctor, my piano teacher; I could walk to the library from Twenty-fifth Street and to the church where I sang in the choir with Nana; and I loved the school I went to and my teacher, Mrs. Jackson—I don't know if she thought I was gifted, but when I showed her the play I had written, she thought it was good enough to have our class put it on for the whole school. But these were not good enough reasons for my mother and she was the one in charge. So she saved up her money and began her search for a house that was "better." That's when we got mixed up in white real estate.

It was on a warm spring evening. My mother had me take my bath early and she combed my hair. She put on lots of hair tonic and braided it tight and then tied the braids with pink ribbons. She put out my Sunday dress for me. It was white with pink flowers and then she told me to put a little Vaseline on the tips of my patent leather shoes. I did what she told me to and squeezed my feet into the shoes, which weren't that old but were already too tight for me.

"Why am I getting all dressed up?" I asked. My mother was getting dressed up, too. She had changed into her Sunday dress also, which was light green linen, and she was putting powder on her cheeks with a powder puff. "Where are we going?"

I asked. She was standing in front of our dresser. I looked up at her face in the mirror.

"House hunting," she said. She carefully painted her lips with her new orange lipstick. The color was called "Tangerine" and went perfectly with her tawny, brown skin and light green dress. Then she dabbed on some perfume. "We're going to meet a lady at a real estate office," she said, smiling down at me. "There's a wonderful-sounding house I read about in the paper."

"How much does it cost?" asked my brother Milton. I hadn't noticed him standing in the doorway. I don't know how long he'd been there. "What's the asking price?" he said. I turned around and stared. Milton was two years younger than me, but he talked like a grown-up man, especially about money.

"I should take you," Mommy said, taking her white sweater out of the bottom drawer. "You're a lot more practical than Sharon is."

Shooting a smirk in my direction, Milton bounced his short frame up onto the edge of my mother's bed. "I'm a lot better at the grocery store," he boasted. "I look at the prices."

I rolled my eyes at him. The one time my mother had sent him shopping instead of me, he'd come back with a lot more groceries in the cart. Ever since then he'd been bragging about what a better shopper he was. I didn't argue, because I knew he was right—he had come back with more groceries. And ever since I'd squandered all of my allowances on Bazooka bubble gum in order to get the wrappers for a "real pearl necklace" that never came, I knew I wasn't very smart with money.

"Where is this house?" Milton nagged. "I hope it's not too expensive."

Mommy patted him on the head. "We definitely can't afford it, but I'm going to look anyway." She blew out a breath and looked up at the ceiling. "Lord have mercy, it has four bed-rooms. I must be crazy. Not only that, it's over there near Chevy Chase."

"Where's that?" I asked.

"Far away from here." She glanced at her watch. "Come on, you kids, let's go check on your brothers." She gave Milton a gentle nudge through the door. "I'll take you next time, Bud. I need you to watch Brian and Georgie."

Downstairs, my two youngest brothers' Brian and Georgie were sitting on the floor in front of the TV watching a rerun of "I Love Lucy." Shortly after we'd moved to Twenty-fifth Street, we'd discovered that the basement leaked, so Mommy had moved the television to the living room next to the piano.

A car horn honked loudly outside. "That's the taxi," Mil-ton announced, striding over to the window. Mommy was kissing Brian and Georgie good-bye. They were a year apart, but were exactly the same size. They also had the same faces, only Brian had blond hair and very pale skin like my father's side of the family, while Georgie had wavy dark hair and dark tan skin like my mother's side. Even though my hair wasn't blond anymore, I had the same pale skin that Daddy and my little brother Brian had. Like Georgie, Milton looked like my mother's side.

"Be good, boys," Mommy said. "Nana will be over to look in on you. I cut up some oranges for a snack and there's a box of vanilla wafers."

My mother and I left. The three boys were waving at the window. The taxi ride to the real estate office didn't take long. Everything about this excursion was a mystery to me; when my mother had bought the house on Twenty-fifth Street, I'd been in the country. Even the word "real estate" had a foreign ring to it.

The agent's name was Mrs. Broadlee. She was wearing a loose-fitting beige outfit made out of a filmy material. Her hair was brown and curled under. Her eyes were gray. She was kind of chubby, like my grandmother in the country, my father's mother. She also had light skin like my grandmother in the country; she had light skin like I had. It never occurred to me that Mrs. Broadlee was a white person. The only white people I'd ever seen were on television, and once you were on television you weren't a person anymore, you were part of a picture on a machine. You weren't exactly "white" either, even if your skin was pale—you were kind of "television" colored. Only when the Negro actors got a part on television did it seem like the people on the screen were actual people—probably because when a Negro got on the television all the grown-ups in the family talked so proud that you'd think the person was in that person's own family. Anyway, Mrs. Broadlee was just a beige nondescript at the moment, because once I was in the back of the car, all I could see was her wide shoulders in the beige outfit. It occurred to me then that Mrs. Broadlee was a pretty good name for her, because her back was so broad.

Up front in the passenger seat, my mother was smiling. The window was rolled down and she was holding onto her hair so that it wouldn't get messed up. I felt very still inside. My toes were hurting inside of my shoes and my braids were pulling my scalp. Then I started sweating. There was something nervous going on in the car, though I couldn't tell what it was.

"The garden has wonderful shrubbery," Mrs. Broadlee was saying in this very fast voice. I saw her looking at me through the rearview mirror. I stared back at her. Then her eyes darted quickly away to my mother.

"Oh, shrubs don't matter much," Mommy said. "I've got three little cowboys at home and I'm allergic to flowers. But Sharon loves anything that grows. Maybe she can be the gardener." Then she shot a glance back at me and gave me a smile. I wiggled my toes and smiled back. I'd been feeling kind of strange all alone in the back with Mrs. Broadlee driving us down this highway I'd never been on before. But when Mommy gave me that look she can give sometimes that said "don't you worry, Sugar—I'm here and I'm in charge" I just about melted with relief. I even got the nerve to say something.

"Are we almost at the house?" I asked.

Mommy looked at Mrs. Broadlee.

"Almost," the broker said. Her voice sounded strange, as if she'd been huffing and puffing. She cleared her throat.

"Your daughter . . . ," she said. She glanced back at me in the rearview mirror.

"What about her?" Mommy asked, smiling.

"Well, she looks . . . uh . . . but your skin. . . Are you part Indian?" The car seemed to be going much faster.

I watched my mother's face. The smile vanished. She straightened her shoulders. "We are Negro," she said calmly, "not Indian."

Mrs. Broadlee changed lanes and pulled off onto the shoulder. "I have to make a stop. I hope you don't mind." Suddenly we were parked at a telephone booth. Cars whizzed by on the highway. I watched Mrs. Broadlee out of the window. She was talking on the phone with someone, covering one side of her face with her hand. I couldn't hear what she was saying. I leaned forward and put my chin on the back of my mother's seat. She didn't turn around or say anything.

"I'm so sorry." Mrs. Broadlee began to speak before she even got back in. She'd poked her head into the window. "I'm so sorry I've put you to so much trouble." She opened the door and slid into the driver's seat.

My mother turned to her. "Is there a problem?"

"I just talked to the owners of the house. I told them that you're colored. They don't want to be the first ones."

"The first ones to what?" My mother sounded tense and angry.

Mrs. Broadlee got a tissue out of her purse and wiped her forehead. "The first ones to sell to Negroes."

She started up the car and made a left onto the highway. I leaned back into my seat. My mother didn't turn around. My toes were hurting again and my back was sweating. Mrs. Broadlee drove us back to the office and we called Capitol Cab for a taxi and then waited outside for it to come. It didn't take long for the brown-faced driver to get there.

"Call for a cab?" he asked, smiling out through the window. Mommy took me by the hand and smiled back.

"Yes, indeed," she said.

We never talked about what had happened that night. Mommy simply told Milton that the house had already been sold when he asked about it. And however she felt about the experience, she didn't give up her search. She was determined to get a better home for us, and for her that meant looking at "white" real estate. I went on at least two other expeditions with her over the next couple of years and hated it. One cold night I remember going into a home with her and my three brothers. Three little white children, dressed for bed, were lined up on the hall stairs. The parents seemed pleasant enough as the broker led us through the house, but after that incident with Mrs. Broadlee I was positive that the family didn't want us to be there. It may have been my imagination, but I thought the little children on the stairs were staring at us as if we were from Mars. The other time I went with her it was a lot more fun—she'd asked a broker to take us to see a house that was practically a mansion with ten rooms, a stone fireplace, and a balcony. We were definitely in fantasy land that day, but my brothers and I had fun running up and down the winding staircase and getting lost in the rooms. Of course the owners had already moved out.

It wasn't until I was in eighth grade that Mommy managed to move out of Anacostia and buy her dream house. Just like the first time, the boys and I had been spending the summer on our grandparents' farm in the country. It was a rough summer for me—I'd developed serious asthma and woke up with my chest heaving every morning. My grandmother made me hot tea and gave me cough syrup, but nothing seemed to help but red-hot peppers on pizza. Even then, when I thought about my dad the wheezing would come right back. It had been three years since he'd bothered to be in touch with us, even during the times when we were with his own parents in the country. When we got home, Mommy drove us to the new house. This time it wasn't a surprise, since she'd written about what she'd done. I think she'd been working out the details before my brothers and I had left, but she hadn't told us. Maybe she was afraid that things at the closing wouldn't work out. At any rate, she'd pulled it off. And the house at 6628 Eastern Avenue, Northwest, was all that she had wanted for us. Downstairs she had a room for herself with her own bathroom. Upstairs there were two other bedrooms, one for me and another that Brian and Georgie would share. Milton would have a small room to sleep in off the basement landing. My room had new furniture in it—actually, it was quite old—Nana and Granddaddy's discarded bedroom set. But it was new for me and quite luxurious. The double bed had a silken comforter with lavender flowers and a long ruffle around the hem. When I walked into my new room, it took my breath away. Other features I loved were the window on the landing, which looked out onto a wonderful garden filled with flowers. The people who had owned the house, whose name was Busby, had been avid gardeners. The front walk and porch were lined with trellises laden with roses and the stone terrace out back was flanked with beds of white peonies which bloomed every spring. Though I was a little old to roll in the leaves, Milton and Georgie could still do it, because the backyard had a slope just like our old one. In the basement there was a large wooden toy chest, which the Busbys had left behind. Even though I'd outgrown toys, I fell in love with the chest instantly. I'd always wanted a toy chest and now I packed this one with all the toys we'd ever owned for my two younger brothers. About six weeks after we moved in, two of the Busby boys, who were now my mother's age, showed up at the door. Their parents had told them that they'd left the toy chest behind in the basement and they wanted to have it for their own children. My mother didn't seem happy about it, but she made us take the toys out and give the chest up. The men weren't very friendly—they never apologized for taking our chest away, nor did they smile at us. Since they were white, I figured that the Busbys had been a white family. So my mother had finally managed to buy her piece of "white" real estate.

My brothers changed schools, but since I was about to graduate from junior high in Southeast, I didn't. I took an hour-and-a-half-long ride on the public bus everyday so that I could move up with my class. And when it came time for high school, I told my mother that I wanted to continue in Southeast and go to Anacostia High with all the kids I'd come up with. Not that I had that many friends or was very popular, but I'd fought hard to make a name for myself. I liked my teachers and knew that I'd learned a lot. I didn't want to risk making a change. It was probably a stupid decision. I could have walked to the high school in my new neighborhood. Anacostia was practically all black—the new school would have been truly integrated. The kids in the new school did things like play tennis in their free time. My friends at Anacostia worked after school, got in trouble, or played basketball. It's hard to describe how different these worlds were—you had to have been there. Anyway, I opted for the old world—the one my mother had worked so hard to get me out of. By the time I finished my extracurriculars and stood at the pitch-black bus stop, most kids were at home eating their dinners. My mother had wanted us out, because it was dangerous; I think it was, but I never felt endangered.

Milton made new friends right away—some of them were white—and became quite popular at the ritzier school. I was so taken up with my teenage life that I kind of lost track of how Brian and Georgie were doing in their new elementary school. By now my mother had a car to go to work in. Ambitious as ever, she was going to school at night to get another degree. She wanted to make more money—there was never enough with four children and everything she wanted for us. But that was the last house.

I never knew the cost of the place on Eastern Avenue, but as I grow older I am more and more aware of the price that she paid for it. Pushing ahead with four children is hard enough—being black and a woman couldn't have made things easier. But for Mommy in some ways it might have, because obstacles fed into her ambition; the harder things were, the more determined she was to try to make a life for us that she considered better. I loved that new piece of real estate. Though I didn't go to school in the neighborhood, I made friends. Two of them were the older Italian couple who lived next door to us, the Grazianos. Mrs. Graziano combed her long white hair in the sun after she washed it and Mr. Graziano taught me how to grow my own tomatoes. Sometimes, however, I wonder whether the new house that the Busbys used to own was worth it. All of my mother's effort went into buying it and into keeping it up. The week before her payday we were always scrambling. Though my brothers may have, I did not take advantage of the mostly white school district it offered. And I'm sure that if we'd stayed in Southeast, Milton still would have become a doctor, Georgie a hospital administrator, and I still would have been a writer. Moving to the "better" neighborhood didn't keep Brian out of trouble or from dying too young. Though I will always remember the view of the white peonies through my favorite window on the landing and always be grateful for the lavender comforter Mommy bought for my new bed, when I think of childhood, I think of the old world. The world of "black" real estate on Twenty-fifth Street. That's the neighborhood I think of, when I think of going back.

Judith Gorog

During a telephone conversation, my friend Ellen asked me if I knew about the wedding cake in the middle of the road. I did not, and settled back, expecting her to tell me. Instead, she said that she had heard that there was a book, a collection of such stories, each by a different writer. I knew nothing of the book, and, frankly, have not spent time looking for it, because Ellen's next question was: What would I do with that image?

Now, I am no good at all at making up stories on the spur of the moment, but that wedding cake was so suggestive that it remained with me, tickling my imagination for days after that telephone conversation. At first, I could see a van hit a bump, the back doors fly open, and the cake slide out onto a city street. So far in my life most of the wedding cakes I have tasted were gross; they looked good, and were no doubt fine for putting under one's pillow to induce dreams of true love to come—but for eating: yuck. So, I imagined a cake that would taste even better than it looked; and I could see children coming from right and left to sample the cake in the middle of the road.

Meanwhile, in the back of my mind were other bits and bites. For example: Aside from the real put-your-fork-into-it cake, there is the symbolic wedding cake, and the symbolic meaning of the road, and of the middle of the road. Roads divide, and join. The middle of the road could be neutral ground, the only place to hold a wedding intended to mend. Marriage, for most of human history, was not about love. It was and is a tool for building or protecting fortunes, land, or power.

Looked at that way, my evolving wedding in the middle of the road could best be described in something like a folktale. The voice I heard was that of an outsider, but she was telling it in the first-person, which is not generally done in a folktale (except in tall tales, of course).

In my telling, I did do something not uncommon in folktales, which is to include snippets from daily life here and now, things a bit incongruous but I hoped amusing. I did that in part because in more than one old tale we are told of kings and queens who speak and act (and perform daily tasks) in ways historians tell us were common to peasants and those who served, not to the ones being served. Or, in an Italian folktale, we hear a story that supposedly takes place in China, but all the details in the story are pure Italy. Those old-time storytellers followed the advice all writers are given: "Write what you know." But, they also worked to satisfy their audience's yearning for the exotic.

I left some mystery in the story. What will become of the narrator? And of the High Judge? I hinted in the story at many things: We know that mediators are necessary, and often at least there is the possibility of the use of force, that peace is fragile and must be tended, that conflicts are not solved but managed, and that doing a good job may not earn praise or love.

Most of the time, when I look at those "story starters" at the end of the questions at the end of the chapters in textbooks, I feel a profound sense of dismay, a complete inability to make up anything, except an excuse to leave. For me, a list of spelling words is quite stimulating, the more wacko the story, and the sentences in it, the better. From the wedding cake in the middle of the road, I discovered that at least once I could make something from a story starter.

The Wedding Cake in the Middle of the Road

I t began with a quarrel that rapidly became a blood feud. The High Judge acted after perfect strangers were murdered when they blundered into our valley. The High Judge ordered, and received, eight kidnapped children, four from each of the two warring clans. Once he had secured the children, he sent to the heads of the two clans a message:

"My army will destroy both your clans. Yes, I know you are so blinded with blood that you will gladly die, every last one of you, so long as all of those you see as enemies also die. That is why I have your children. I alone will decide, after all of you are dead, who will be the lone, and lonely, survivor of this dreadful, and remarkably stupid, conflict. Know as you perish that the child, and the generations, of your enemy will outlive you.

"If, however, you wish to enjoy the springtime next year, then send to me your sons and daughters of marriageable age. I will choose the two whose marriage will seal the end of this blood feud. I will choose the place and the time and will make a marriage feast your great-grandchildren will praise in song and dance."

I did not tell the High Judge that my family would count only three children as hostages. Nobody would count me; that's why I was so easy to kidnap.

His Honor; that's what he told me to call him, clapped his hands together, as he paced his chambers after the messengers galloped off to deliver the words. I was trying to read, but he kept asking me words for his crossword puzzle, and then arguing with whatever I suggested. He had put the other children into a schoolroom and playground, with a strong-armed teacher to stop any fighting. From what I heard, it was peaceful. The kids were glad to be out of danger, to be fed and warm, and in a place full of things to do. The blood feud had made life pretty miserable at home, spoiling crops and harvests, and making the grown-ups bad-tempered when they were well, and terrifying when they were dying of their wounds.

"There will be a truce," the Judge told me, "and the first thing I want you to do is to go over to that hillside. See it over there?"

Once again I had to put down my book and go over to the telescope at the chamber window. I found the hillside and asked why I had to go over there. The Judge slapped his hands together in annoyance while he explained that I had to go there with a trowel and a bag of daffodil bulbs because some idiot had planted a single bulb every three feet on that hillside, which was not the idea of naturalizing at all, but more like a cemetery. He told me I had to get myself over there and plant two or four or even five bulbs near every one that was blooming because he could not stand to look at the hillside for the twenty years it would take nature to make beautiful that planting.

And so, once the group of marriageable youth arrived, I went off with a donkey and a sack of bulbs, and a trowel, and spent the cool hours of the day digging and planting. Even though I knew His Honor was watching through the telescope, I sat under a tree on the top of the hill through all the hot hours of midday and read my book in peace.

It was the story of a girl who had been kidnapped by a band of starving bandits. They planned to roast and eat her, but she started a story they had never heard, so they decided to wait until she finished it before killing her. It is two hundred pages now, all pretty good stories, mostly of ghosts and things, never about food. I wonder how she will escape, but I had to leave the hillside after the last bulb was planted. It is the wrong time of year to plant daffodils, but I did not tell the High Judge that.

Ah, in the weeks since the truce, I have come to see that His Honor certainly knows how to accomplish the tasks he sets. Horoscopes have been cast, and the perfect couple discovered. Their marriage will cement the peace. I don't know who they are yet. The Judge has put them somewhere, with matchmakers and chaperones and seamstresses, and heaven knows who else, to make everything ready in time.

The way he is clapping his hands and muttering, I can tell the High Judge is debating whether he should have another five or six well-matched couples marry, as insurance. I think that is why he has ordered that the young people remain here. He told them it is to practice their gymnastics and dancing until the wedding. He has sent home all the other children he ordered kidnapped but is keeping me here.

He has a job for me. I wonder what it is.

How strange this thing is, the one we call Fate. I was born of a servant girl everyone in the family says was too ugly ever to marry. No man in our clan has ever stepped forward to claim me as his child. My poor mother died at my birth, and I certainly would have followed her if another poor woman had not felt pity for me. She too died, just after I had begun to follow after her on my own feet. The whole family calls me an unlucky child, and ugly to boot. My skin is the wrong color, and my hair the wrong texture, and I say things everyone finds strange. Mostly I keep quiet, and mostly I keep out of the way, but sometimes I forget to pay attention. I should most probably have been killed during the bloody part of that long blood feud, but I was overlooked. The High Judge's soldiers found me easily, and thought me a good catch because I was reading and was dressed in fine clothes. The reading and the clothes were accidents. I taught myself to read when I was small, and the clothes were rejected by everyone because my cousin who wore them killed herself for love. They said she was bewitched. She saw a boy from the "enemy" clan and fell in love through her eyes. He was the wrong one then, and now I have learned he is the groom in the wedding-to-be. What if my poor unlucky cousin had not killed herself? Would her horoscope have been the right one for him? I suppose not. I will not cast it now. It is too late for her. Me? The High Judge has ordered me to plan the wedding. Everything about it must symbolize the peace to follow.

First of all, I must select the place. The date and hour have been chosen to be fortunate. The High Judge assures me, after criticizing my word. How can he criticize? He asked for seven letters meaning "pinched," and I said "topiary," and he said that one put plants in fantastic shapes by chopping, cropping, or twisting and cutting, and I said you could pinch them if they were tender enough plants, and he went off muttering.

I walked back to the valley. The road is dirt, which means it is muddy in the springtime, and dusty in the summer. There are houses, three of them, from our clan on one side of the road, but set back behind gardens. On the other side of the road, also set back, way back, behind gardens and behind walnut trees that are green this year for the first time since the fighting began, are two houses belonging to the other clan. I walked a long time today, looking for the right spot for the wedding, and for the reasons for the spot. I returned to the High Judge at nightfall. I could see the telescope eye moving. He had been watching for me. We ate supper while I told him of my wedding plans. I believe he likes them. Back from the road, far back in the hills on both sides, are the stone houses of the rest of the members of the two clans. They have small farms, and herds of sheep, goats, and cattle, which they take high in the mountains to summer pasture.

The invitations and the orders have been sent. Every family is to bring from home their second-best rug, and their largest table and cloth.

It is the day. From the household of the High Judge came a wagon with a mysterious load. It was covered. He did not tell me what it contained. I directed that the carpets be placed on the dust of the road. They covered it and extended to the grass on both sides. The tables are set, and the feast laid out. The musicians have assembled.

Three groups played together at first, one from each clan, and the best ones from the household of the High Judge. They then played in succession for the dancing and singing, which went on for three days. The feast was food for a year, and a wedding cake taller than a man. The cake sat on a table set upon the most beautiful of the carpets, one of deep red, "blood-red," the High Judge says, accented with the blue and black of the night sky.

The three days were bright with sunshine, cooled by a breeze that barely stirred the grass and leaves. The time for the first ceremony was set for afternoon. The days are long, and the evenings pleasant. Still, for that wedding cake in the middle of the road, I had made a canopy to shade it. There were colored flowers of sugar, and real ones too. The bees buzzed from one to the other. The children passed by to admire and to taste where their fingers could reach. There was enough to eat of this cake, and enough to take for the dreams it creates when kept in a special place while you sleep.

I told the celebrants that we could not sit under the trees because of the many caterpillars crawling on and dropping from the walnut trees on one side, and from the peach trees on the other. The families from the other clan were at first bewildered at the coldness of my own clan to my directions. I think at first they assumed it was because I am so young, but they soon questioned my every direction just as my own people did.

The Judge was correct. There was first the wedding to end the quarrel and cement the peace, and then five more weddings we can hope will ensure the future of the peace. The whole was celebrated without a harsh word, with dance and song. That youth for whom my cousin killed herself looked besotted with his bride, and she with him, and I told myself not to think anything that could bring bad luck. At the end of the feast the High Judge told each family to choose a rug from the middle of the road, but not the one they brought.

There was some problem with his words. I could tell, and if I had known he would say them, I should have warned him. From pride and the desire to make this wedding feast great, some families did not bring their second-best rug, but the best they owned. It obviously pained them to leave it in the middle of the road. Heads bowed, each chose a rug. I feared the peace would be undone by that dratted Judge. But he then went to his wagon and ordered it uncovered. To each family he gave a rug of surpassing beauty and quality, far far better than what any of us had owned before this day.

"Now think on these rugs," he told them. "Think on the one you gave for this feast with all your goodwill, and think on the ones you take home. Think when your great-grandchildren crawl on them and when they sing of this day."

After it was done and dark, I stood in the middle of the road, in my fine dress the Judge had ordered to surprise me on this day. I looked at the patterns the rugs, and the feet of humans, animals, and tables had left in the dust of the road. I also thought that I should put one of my feet in front of the other, right foot, left foot, until I had followed the road right out of the valley.

"This is, at this time, not the place for you." It was the High Judge speaking out of the darkness, and it startled me. I thought he had left with ceremony and music long before the tables were cleared. "Come. Before we know it, both sides will find fault with the wedding arrangements. You have always been an outsider, which is why I wanted you to make the wedding. Tomorrow or after tomorrow we will send you to the university to study. In a few years you will make an excellent High Judge, and in the meantime, what is an eight-letter word that is the opposite of 'mendacity'?"

"I might say 'kindness,' but you would say 'truthful,' " I replied.

"That is because lying is not always unkind, which you may or may not learn at the university," said the High Judge, walking very fast down the middle of the road. Because there was a bit of a sugar flower on the fold, I could see that he had wrapped a piece of wedding cake in a napkin.

Neal Shusterman

When I was in college, my girlfriend and I played this weird little game. We took a few pictures of ourselves, then held the photos side by side, and crossed our eyes until the two images came together. We kept our eyes crossed until our brains, rather than showing us two juxtaposed images, finally gave up and morphed the two images into one, and we could get a glimpse of what our children might look like someday.

Now that I think about it, that's an interesting concept for a story in and of itself . . . but that's not the tale I'm telling here. I mention it because, to me, writing is a lot like taking different images, juxtaposing them over one another, and seeing what happens. I very rarely write from a single experience. More than likely I take several experiences, stick them together, and create a whole that is hopefully greater than the sum of the parts. *The Eyes of Kid Midas*, for example, came about because of a cool pair of shades I had when I was seventeen, that made me feel invincible, overlaid by a camping trip I once took to a bizarre rock formation called "The Devil's Punchbowl."

This story takes two situations that actually occurred, with two different friends . . . but when I began crossing my mind's eye, and saw the two situations dissolving into each other, I realized the story became more interesting, and took on greater poignancy. There are other experiences as well, folded into "Blue Diamond," from a trip to an amusement park when I was thirteen, to a recent trip to Las Vegas I took to research my book *Thief of Souls*.

As for what's real, and what's not, well, all of it really happened in one way or another. I was hijacked, by a crazy friend, to Las Vegas when I was seventeen, and a year or two later I had to save another friend's life at three in the morning. And the blue diamond—well, my friend bought it from the guy in the parking lot, not me. I was the one who was freaking, figuring the two shady guys in the Cadillac were about to relieve us of our lives. Turns out, in real life, that the diamond was a fake, and worth about fifty bucks, so my friend became one of those suckers that are reported to be born every minute. (Serves him right for kidnapping me just before midterms.)

And incidentally, I married that girlfriend who mind-morphed photos with me. We have two kids, and neither of them resembles our photo-morphs. But there's a third one on the way, so you never know. . . .

Blue Diamond

Quiet Saturday evening. My parents took my sister to the movies so I can slave away in peace at the kitchen table. TV off. Stereo shut down. Quiet Saturday evening. Until Quinn comes by.

"Dude, you're gonna study yourself to death," says Quinn.

I turn a page in my algebra book. "Math midterm on Monday," I tell him. "My parents are gonna be pissed if I don't pull down a decent grade."

Quinn shakes his head, grimacing, as if the mere thought of studying was something horrific. "They ride you too hard, Doug."

"It's all right," I tell him. "I'll get 'em back by getting into some super-expensive Ivy League school they'll have to take out a mortgage to pay for."

He shrugs at that. We're both finishing up our junior year of high school, but I get the feeling he's not college bound—which is weird, because his whole family has degrees coming out of their ears. Parents, sisters, brothers—he's the fifth kid in his family—which is why they named him Quinn.

Quinn flings open the refrigerator, and looks for something to plunder. But my Dad's on a diet, which means that the proverbial cupboard is bare, not to mention the fridge. We all lose weight when Dad's on a diet, whether we want to or not.

Quinn closes the refrigerator hard enough to dislodge a magnet or two. "How can you study without brain food?" he asks. "Whadaya say we go get something to eat."

"Gotta study," I tell him, trying my best to focus on the list of equations on the page.

"So, bring your book with you."

I can see Quinn's having one of his "What-about-me" moments. He's bored, he's got nothing to do, and so the whole world has to put down whatever it happens to be doing just to entertain Quinn. I know he won't leave me alone until he gets his way, and I figure I could do with a short break. I mark my place in the textbook as I close it, fully believing that I'll get back to it later that night. Call me an optimist. Or call me a moron.

Quinn drives his dad's new Lexus. His dad *never* lets Quinn drive the Lexus—he even locks the steering wheel with "The Car Club" just to keep Quinn away from it.

So much for antitheft devices. Quinn weaves skillfully through traffic on Harbor Boulevard. He drives kind of the same way he walks through crowds—suddenly, skillfully darting to the left or right to avoid people and objects in his way as if his whole life is just the negotiation of a maze. I've gotta admit, it's a trip being in his wake. You never quite know what off-the-wall thing he's going to do next. Me, I'm about as predictable as a traffic light—which is probably why we've been such good friends since grade school. He keeps me from turning into a drone, and I keep him from sailing off into the stratosphere. It's what we call in science a "symbiotic" relationship.

A thin crescent moon shines through the sun roof, cold and sharp as a scythe. Before us the Boulevard lights fly by, as we talk about girls, sports, and global warming . . . and then I notice that we've passed all the usual fast-food places. I ask Quinn what gives.

"I don't feel like the usual stuff tonight. I need a place with atmosphere," he says. "Let's go to Planet Hollywood—I'll buy."

Before I can answer, he pulls across four lanes, to make a well-orchestrated but totally maniacal left turn. I glance at the little airbag symbol on the dashboard in front of me, for reassurance. "Well, okay . . . if you're buying."

As we speed down the freeway, it occurs to me that Quinn has never offered to buy. He even used to make his dates pay for their meals until I convinced him that that was sick and twisted. I begin to wonder if, perhaps, he's gotten a part-time job or something, so that now he can squander his own money instead of just his parents'.

We miss the turnoff for Planet Hollywood. From my window I can see it's neon globe orbiting past us.

"Nice one, Quinn." And I begin to feel a bit edgier than usual. Perhaps because Quinn didn't even try to fly across like a million lanes of traffic to make the exit at the last second. Instead he just held the wheel steady, staring forward with an unreadable expression on his face.

"It's okay," he says. "Actually I think there's another one."

"Where?"

"Just down the road a bit."

But I know of no other Planet Hollywood nearby. "Where down the road?"

He hesitates a moment, then he finally says, "Las Vegas."

It hits me slowly, like a kick to the groin. It takes a few moments until I get the full impact. This is not a study break, this is a road trip, at the worst possible time, in the worst possible way.

"No!" I tell him flatly. "No, Quinn, you're not going to do this! It's crazy, even for you."

But he only grins, and I know that he had planned this all along.

"I'm getting out," I threaten.

"So get out," he says, but makes no move to slow down the car. Then, in what must be a flash of sinister inspiration, he picks up the car phone, and leaves a message for my parents. "I've kidnapped Doug for his own good," Quinn says into the phone. "He'll be back sometime tomorrow. 'Bye."

Realizing that my algebra book is in the trunk, inaccessible until Quinn chooses to stop the car, I bring my hands to my face as if covering my eyes can make this all go away. Well, all right, I have to admit, beneath the layers of worry, there's a small part of me that's excited as hell—after all I've never been to Las Vegas . . . but the thing is, I know Quinn well enough to know that he's lying. This trip isn't for *my* own good—it's got something to do with him. This is more than his usual restlessness. A four-hundred-mile road trip isn't powered by boredom and nervous energy. There's something else squirreling around through his head.

"You know, your parents are gonna kill you," I tell him.

"Not if I do the job first," he says.

For a moment I wonder what possessed him to say that, but then he cranks up the stereo, and it blows any thoughts I have out through the open sun roof.

Desert night, loud and glaring. A massive black pyramid to our left, probably larger than the real ones, and the sprawling emerald cathedral of the MGM Grand to our right. Quinn pulls into the valet, like some high roller.

"Are you supposed to tip the valet on the way in or on the way out?" He asks me, as if I have any idea, then says "Who cares?" and gives the valet five bucks without a second thought. I notice there's a whole wad of bills in his usually empty wallet.

"What, did some old relative die and leave you a fortune?"

"Been saving up," was all he says, then he hands me a fifty. "Here," he said. "For the casino. You'll owe me."

"Yeah, like forever," I say, but I keep the fifty anyway, shoving good old Grant deep into my pocket.

Terrified that I'll get thrown into some seedy Las Vegas jail for being underage, I move cautiously through the MGM casino. In a hidden corner, I dump some change into a slot machine. Three lion's heads on my first pull. Ultimate beginner's luck. *Ching-ching-ching-ching-ching.* Two machines down, a pasty, painted old woman with a cigarette glued to her lip grunts in disapproval. I collect my winnings, and seek out Quinn, who has just found a suitable blackjack table. In certain light, Quinn could pass for twenty-one . . . but this isn't the light. The second he sits down, the pit boss asks him for identification.

Quinn wastes no time. He does one of his evasive maneuvers, and we exit stage left from this particular MGM production.

The story's the same beneath the shining minarets of Excaliber, and the miniaturized skyscrapers of New York New York. ID talks; snot noses walk.

Quinn's face begins to narrow into a frustrated scowl as we get back into the car. Actually, I'm figuring this is a good thing, because how much money can you lose if no one lets you play?

. . . But leave it to Quinn to find some rundown dive where

no one seems to know the difference between seventeen and twenty-one—not even the blackjack dealers.

We sit beside a drunk construction cowboy, at a stained blackjack table, five-dollar minimum. Seems like adding cards is as close as I'll come to algebra tonight.

I win, Quinn loses. Big. An hour later, I walk off with two hundred bucks, not to mention the bulge of coins still in my pocket, and Quinn's wallet is empty.

And yet he doesn't seem to care. He heads toward a cash machine in the corner, and swipes a credit card through. His mother's card. About now I begin to feel guilty. After all, I'm supposed to be Quinn's safety net, right? I shouldn't have let him blow all his cash at that table. The thing is, I was having too good a time watching them take away his chips, and pile up mine. I grab his hand before he can enter the credit card's PIN number.

"Hey Quinn, maybe you should—"

But he shakes my hand off of him. Not just shakes it, but hurls it. Violently. "Just leave me alone, I know what I'm doing."

He enters the number, and punches in two hundred dollars. I can't believe it. "What's wrong with you? Your parents'll ground you off the face of the earth!"

"Yeah, but I won't *be* on the face of the earth."

Long silence as I try to fathom what he's trying to tell me.

"What's that supposed to mean?"

He plucks the money from the machine, and gauges his own answer before saying it out loud. "Exactly what you think it means," he says. "And if you don't believe me check the glove-compartment."

Half an hour later we're back in the car. I had watched, feeling helpless and useless as Quinn threw chips randomly down on a roulette table. All two hundred dollars gone in thirty minutes. I don't know what to think. I don't know what weird head game Quinn is pulling, and why he chose tonight to pull it.

What he said—maybe it's just a joke, I think. He's always dredging up practical jokes, from the pit of his eccentric soul and sometimes they go too far. Like the time he staged that car accident on April Fools' Day, when all the victims, before the angry eyes of police and paramedics, jumped up and started singing the National Anthem. But it was an unspoken rule that Quinn never pulled jokes on me.

He continues driving down the Strip. Not weaving the way he usually drives, but patient with the impossible traffic, as if he's in no hurry to get anywhere in particular.

Again I look to the little airbag emblem on the dashboard in front of me . . . and then to the little release button just beneath it.

The glove compartment.

Before I lose my nerve, I reach out, push the button, and the little door pops open to reveal the car registration in one corner, and in the other corner a small black revolver. This is not April Fools'. I shudder and slam the glove compartment closed so I don't have to see it anymore. Quinn just stares ahead.

"So roulette's not good enough for you?" I force out. "Now you have to play Russian Roulette?"

Quinn shakes his head. "Naah. All the chambers are loaded."

I don't bother to look. I believe him, although I wish I didn't. Of all the things I want to do and say, only one makes it to the surface. "Why . . . ?"

He shrugs it off like it's little more than cutting class. "It's just something I have to do." He glances at me almost grinning. "Lighten up—it's not like I'm gonna do it right in front of you or anything. Hell, I might not even use the thing, if I come up with a better way."

"So why am I here? Am I supposed to come up with your 'better way'? Because you can forget it."

"Don't be dumb. You're here because I can't have a good time in Las Vegas alone, and I'm gonna have a damn good time tonight. So let's just keep having fun. Okay?"

"Yeah. Yeah sure." I say, wondering what part of this he defines as fun. I want to talk to him. I want to start some conversation that will somehow get me into that brain of his so I can decipher what's going on in there. But all I can say is, "Where are we going now?"

He points up ahead, where a slender white tower rises more than a hundred stories up off the Strip. "The Stratosphere Tower," he says. "I hear it's a real trip!"

A thousand and eighty feet in the air, we ride a roller coaster that flies around the top of the Stratosphere, threatening to eject its passengers into an unpleasant sky dive. When I was ten, it was Quinn who taught me that roller coasters are much more fun when your hands are up in the wind . . . but today I grip the safety bar tight, and watch Quinn hurling up his hands, daring the ride to send him flying. He's a roller coaster himself—maybe that's why he likes them so much. There are times when he's flying on so much energy, you can't help but be caught up in whatever he's doing. Then there are the times he's so down on everything you just want to shove him under a rock until he has something pleasant to say. Sometimes when its really bad he disappears for a few days into his room.

So, he's manic-depressive. I know that, I'm not an idiot. But no matter what he thinks, it's not a reason to blow his own brains out.

The coaster rolls around the tower again, and as I watch Quinn, it occurs to me the real reason why he brought me here. It wasn't just to keep him company, whether he knows it or not.

After the ride, we stand together on the observation deck, the air remarkably still for this height. It's two in the morning, and the city below shines as bright as day. Quinn glances up at the guard railing. He tests the fence with his hands. I know what he's thinking.

"Hey listen," I say, "once you've aced yourself, do you think I could have your CD collection?"

He snaps his eyes to me, caught completely off guard by the request. Then he shrugs. "Sure, I guess."

"Good. You don't mind if I sell the ones I don't like, do you?"

He lets go of the fence. "You're gonna break up my collection?"

"Face it, Quinn—nobody in the world is gonna want some of those weird groups you've got."

"They're great groups!" he insists.

"Yeah—and you know what?" I lean a bit closer to him. "You're never going to hear a single one of them ever again."

I can see the thought beginning a little volley in his head.

"What's that group you like so much? 'Blanco Bronco'? Didn't you say they have a new album coming out this month?"

"Next month."

I raise an eyebrow. "Tough break."

It's not like his resolve really wavers. It's just that I had thrown something new into the equation. Granted, it was a small thing, but still he has to factor it in—and when it comes to factoring equations, studying or not, I could wipe the floor with Quinn.

"Nice try," he says to me with steely eyes. Then he heads inside without looking back at the fence.

Four A.M. We sit in Circus Circus, watching a bad Country-Western group perform in a lounge for a crowd of five. We don't order any drinks, so no one bothers to kick us out. I squirm silently, nervously, trying to think of a million ways to stop him. Meanwhile, Quinn's looking more and more with-drawn, as he feels his own time running down. Did he think he could fit a whole lifetime into a twelve-hour spree?

He takes a deep breath after the most godawful song. "Gotta use the bathroom," he says. He gets up, and, since I'm feeling exhaustion set in, I don't go with him.

Then about twenty seconds after he leaves, I realize he might not be going to the bathroom at all. How could I be so stu-pid!

Panicked, I stumble over the cocktail table, and race off to find the bathrooms, praying that he's in there just taking a piss.

I fly into the bathroom, and my heart sinks. He's not there. There's just a fat man in a plaid jacket drying his hands with one of those electric hand dryers. "Don't you hate these things," the man says to me.

A stall opens and out steps Quinn. He looks at the way I'm huffing and puffing like I just ran the hundred-meter. He can only meet my eyes for an instant before looking away as he washes his hands. "What's your problem?"

"Just don't do that again," I tell him. "Don't just walk off."

He doesn't answer me.

"C'mon," he says, "nothing left here." He dries his hands on his pants, and strolls out. I match his pace, not following in his wake anymore, but walking alongside him. It's easy to do that, now that he's moving straight, no longer darting in and out. Now I realize that, in spite of all pretensions, today isn't one of his manic days. He's not depressed either. He's somewhere in between. I guess that in-between can be just as dangerous.

The Lexus is parked in a bleak parking garage. The place is desolate, with half its lights burned out. I make sure he lets me in first, so he can't get in and leave me there to go do his final business alone.

He puts the key in the ignition, but turns it just far enough to get power to the windows, which he rolls down, letting in the chilly night air. He doesn't turn on the engine. Instead he just watches the keychain swing back and forth, until it comes to rest.

"So what now?" I dare to ask.

He still won't look at me. I can hear the cartilage gulp of his Adam's apple as he swallows. "This is harder than I thought."

"You know I won't let you go through with it."

"You can't follow me into every bathroom."

It's a truth that hits home, and this time it's me that has to look away.

Quinn takes the keys out of the ignition, and fiddles with them for a moment, buying time by connecting each key to some lock four hundred miles away.

"Sometimes," he begins, "sometimes the world feels like this black hole, and I'm just sort of skating around the edge. There's lots of times I feel like I'm falling in." And then finally he looks at me. "Unless you've been there, you can't imagine how awful it feels."

I could try to console him by telling him that I have been there, but the truth is, I haven't—and maybe he's right. Maybe I can't imagine that.

"Anyway," he says, "I never want to be there again."

He takes a quick glance at the glove compartment, and then back at me. Yeah, I know why he had me come on this trip.

He needs me to stop him—to be his safety net for the biggest drop of all. But what can I say to him that will make that black place any less real? I could try to convince him what an awful world this would be without him . . . after all we've both seen *It's a Wonderful Life*, right? But in the here-and-now that just doesn't ring true. The world would not be worse off without him. It wouldn't be better off either. It would just . . . be.

A car comes screeching around a bend in the parking garage seizing our attention. It's an old beat-up car. Big one. Some Cadillac relic from the seventies. It screeches to a halt. Inside are two guys that look like they're straight from a post office mug shot. It is the classic prelude to a mugging. Or a murder.

The bald driver peers at us with rheumy bovine eyes, and the stringy-haired guy riding shotgun leans way out of his window, shouting at Quinn through our open window.

"Hey, buddy, wanna buy a diamond."

Quinn is caught entirely off guard. His jaw bobs up and down, but says nothing. He fumbles to get the key back into the ignition, but before he can, the guy is out of the Cadillac and leaning into the window, with a little velvet bag.

"See, I won it playing poker the other day," he tells us. "But I owe big bucks to bad people, if you know what I mean. They won't take the diamond—they want cash . . . I gotta get some now."

He tilts the bag, and out rolls a perfect blue diamond. At least three carats. It glitters even in the dim lights of the garage. "It's worth a few thousand, but I'll take whatever I can get."

"No thanks," says Quinn. Again he reaches to turn the ignition. I'm not exactly sure what comes over me in the instant. Perhaps it's that look of terror on Quinn's face. I want that look to stay—just long enough to snap him back away from the edge he's been talking about.

"Wait a minute," I say, pulling the keys from the ignition. "I want to see the diamond."

The stringy-haired guy throws Quinn the evilest evil eye I'd ever seen. "I'm going to talk to your friend," he says, then comes around to the other side of the car.

"What are you, nuts?" Quinn whispers to me. "Are you totally insane?"

"You betcha!" I whisper back.

The guy shoves his hand through my window and let me examine the diamond. "I'm desperate, man. What'll you give me for it. A thousand? Eight hundred?"

I grab my wallet and pull out the two hundred I won.

The guy starts to look seriously distressed. "Aw c'mon! Two hundred? This is the real thing here—see?" Then he takes the diamond and drags a broad stroke right across the windshield. It leaves a foot-long scar in the glass. "See? Only a diamond can do that!"

Quinn just looked at the scratch in horrific disbelief. "He scratched the windshield with a diamond," he mutters. "My father's gonna kill me."

I hold out my wad of bills to the scuzzy guy. "Two hundred. It's all I've got. Take it or leave it."

He gives me an evil eye, but not quite as evil as the one he gave Quinn. "Fine. Give me the money." I hand him the cash, and he gives me the diamond. "There. If you got a girlfriend it'll make her real happy . . . and if you don't it'll get you one."

Then he hops back into the Caddy with his cow-faced friend, and they blast into hyperspace once more, leaving Quinn and me alone with one blue diamond.

I give Quinn back the keys, and he starts the car, speeding us out of the lonely garage, and into the bright lights of the predawn strip.

I roll the diamond around in my fingers, watching how it catches the colorful lights around us.

"You're crazy!" announces Quinn. "Those guys could have killed us!"

Of course he's right. It was a stupid, impulsive thing for me to do. But there was a victory in that. For both of us.

"We had a revolver to defend ourselves," I remind him.

"Oh, yeah, that's real smart. Pull out the revolver and get blown away by sawed-off shotguns."

I have to smile at Quinn's reaction. Usually it's me chiding him for being a grade-A lunatic. It's good, for once, to see it turned around. And it's even better to see him heading toward the interstate. It means there's one thing I know he won't be doing tonight.

"You don't really believe that guy's story, do you?" Quinn asks. "I mean, the diamond's probably stolen, or it's a fake."

"Probably."

"So what did you buy it for."

"I didn't buy it for me, I bought it for you." I toss the diamond into his lap. He swerves a bit as he tries to retrieve it from the seat.

"What are you talking about?"

"If the guy's story is for real, then you've got yourself one hell of a diamond," I tell him. "If it's stolen, I'll bet there's a reward when you turn it in—and if it's a fake, big deal. It wasn't my money I gave him anyway—it was the casino's." Then I smile. "You gotta be just a little bit curious about it. When we get home, you should take it to a jeweler and get it checked out."

Quinn throws me a resigned glance, that also seems tinged with gratitude as well. Not for the diamond . . . but for the fact that I've managed to head him home. As we merge on the interstate, I turn to see dawn break over the palaces of Las Vegas, lights still burning, refusing to be outdone by the rising sun.

"This stupid diamond isn't much of a reason, you know," says Quinn. "Tomorrow, I'm gonna be back in the same place."

"Blanco Bronco," I remind him. "You gotta hang around to hear their new album next month. Promise me that much."

I can practically hear Quinn adding time to his personal clock, like coins to a parking meter. "And then what?"

"Isn't your sister due in a few months?" I suggest. "You're gonna be an uncle. Promise me you'll be here long enough to be an uncle."

Quinn shakes his head. "It's all little reasons. Don't you get it, I can't find any big reasons."

"Maybe there *are* no big reasons. Maybe people stay alive because there's seventy years' worth of little reasons all lined up one after another." And then I ask him again. "So promise me you'll be here to be an uncle."

He thinks about it for a long moment, then nods decisively. Another coin in the meter. "Yeah. Okay. I can promise that."

Then he becomes quiet and darkly pensive. I begin to worry about the things that might be going through his mind . . . until he says, "My parents are gonna go nuts on me when I get home."

We both think about that, and, strangely enough we begin to laugh, because that seems so microscopically unimportant now. In a few moments, we're caught in an uncontrollable fit of giggles—the kind that comes when you've been awake for twenty-four hours.

"I can't wait to see the look on my dad's face," says Quinn, "when he sees that diamond scratch on the windshield!"

And we lose it again, laughing until our sides begin to ache . . . because now getting back home—both the good and the bad of it—has become something to look forward to.

Avi

This story is based on something that did in fact happen to me. When coming home from a neighborhood dance held at a church, I was surrounded and beaten up by a gang of boys. My father's response is not unlike what you will read here. I used some aspects of this experience in a book, *A Place Called Ugly*, which I wrote some years ago.

Having said that, this work is a piece of fiction. Only the bare outline of the events—as I experienced them—are to be found here. I am not Charlie. My father is not Mr. Biderbik. Much of what you will read has been imagined.

Readers often confuse what is real and unreal in an author's work. A safe rule of thumb is to suggest that all of the emotions are based on personal experiences, but very few of the events are.

Paula Fox, one of our finest writers, has suggested that the "writer's job is to imagine the truth." I rather like that. I would only add that writers can only imagine the truth if they are honest with their own reality. And that is not as easy as it sounds. Try it.

Biderbiks Don't Cry

Charlie Biderbik stood before the mirror in his room brushing back his thick, dark hair. He wasn't considering what he was doing or even how he looked. He was thinking about the fall dance that night at St. Anne's

Episcopal Church, fifteen city blocks away. Run by the church for neighborhood kids, the event was held four times a year. Anyone between the ages of thirteen and eighteen could go as long as they didn't smoke, drink, or make trouble. Charlie—who was fourteen—was not likely to do any of that, which was why he was uneasy about going.

When his school had a class party or a dance, Charlie went and enjoyed himself. But those were small affairs. He knew the faces. He knew the chaperones. He felt comfortable. He could—and did—have a good time.

The dance at St. Anne's promised to be different. It would be big. Not only had he never gone before, he would only know a few kids. But a real band was promised.

Actually the only reason he was going was because Alice VanGert had suggested he come. Alice was a classmate and Charlie liked her a lot. Not that he had ever told her. As far as she was concerned, they were just friends.

During the past week they had talked in school, and she casually mentioned she was going to the dance with a bunch of friends. "Why don't you come?" she said.

Blushing, he said he probably would go. How could he say no?

When he mentioned the dance to his best friend, Arlo, and suggested they go together, Arlo shook his head. "No way I'm going," Arlo said.

"Why?"

"Lot of rough stuff at those dances."

Charlie felt instant alarm. "Like what?"

"Like gangs."

"That true?"

"Hey, man, would I tell you a lie?"

Charlie never felt he was a brave person. When it came to things like fighting, or any kind of violence, he shrank from it. Just the thought of it made him tense. Not that he ever told anyone. Not even Arlo. Moreover, he was convinced that if people found out about it, they would mock him, reject him. Most of the time it was not something he had to deal with. But now there was Alice, the dance, and his promise that he would go.

Charlie went to the kitchen where his mother—who had just gotten home from work—was preparing dinner.

He said, "Thought I'd go to the dance at St. Anne's tonight."

"That's nice."

"But . . . uh . . . I don't know if I should."

"Why's that?"

"Arlo said there would be gangs there."

Mrs. Biderbik paused in her work to look around at Charlie with anxious eyes. "Maybe," she said, "you should talk to your father first. He'll be home soon."

Charlie believed in his father as he believed in no one else. It wasn't because his father was a successful lawyer whom people called continually for advice. Or that—as he once explained to Charlie—he was the head of the family with the responsibility to solve problems and organize them all. Or that Mr. Biderbik had been a champion college boxer. It was all of those things, together.

Yet there were times—even as Charlie adored his father— that he feared him. There was no fear of anything physical. No, what Charlie feared was that his father would think poorly of him, consider him in some way a failure.

Shortly after six Mr. Biderbik returned home from work. He was a big man, six-foot-three, broad-chested. Tie askew and pulled down, he sat on the edge of his highback wooden chair with a beer can in hand. His shirt collar was open. His wide shoulders were thrust forward, giving him a powerful presence.

His face was swarthy so that even though he had shaved that morning he was in need of another shave. His shaggy eyebrows were equally dark and seemed to have been made to protect eyes which were gray, the color of the sea.

No one seeing them side by side could fail to notice that they were father and son. Everyone said that. They also said that Charlie was going to grow up to be just like his father. There was the same dark complexion, the same heavyset body, the same pale eyes. But there was some hint—Charlie's large feet—that the boy would be bigger than his father. That was a notion Charlie could hardly imagine. But as for being like his father . . . It was all that Charlie wished.

"What's up, pal?" his father said. "You look worried."

Charlie, standing before his father, shifted uncomfortably on his feet. "It's about a dance, at St. Anne's," he began. "Tonight."

"Sounds good to me."

"Yeah. I was thinking of going. But they said that there might be gangs there."

"Gangs at the dance?" his father repeated. "At the church?" He had a habit of repeating information by way of absorbing it. It was a way—Mr. Biderbik had instructed Charlie—of absorbing facts, of thinking on his feet. . . .

"Yes, sir."

A faint smiled hovered over Mr. Biderbik's lips. "How many . . . gangs?"

"I don't know. Two, one."

That time Mr. Biderbik did smile. "Charlie, try to be precise. A sloppy mind muddies the world."

Charlie, flustered, said, "One then."

"Who told you? Fact? Rumor? Gossip?"

Charlie shrugged. "Kids."

"Someone in particular?"

"Arlo."

"Ah, Arlo." Charlie sensed disapproval. Arlo wasn't the neatest of kids. His father liked neatness.

"Yeah."

"How does Arlo know?"

Charlie shrugged.

"Has he been to one of these dances?"

"I . . . don't think so."

As if he were addressing a jury, Mr. Biderbik jabbed at the air. "So he doesn't know for certain?"

Charlie, suddenly sensing it was a waste of time to differ with his father, gave up. "I guess he doesn't know."

Mr. Biderbik smiled at his son. Then he said, "You want to go to the dance, don't you?"

"Yes, sir."

"But what you're saying is that there's a risk, a small risk, that something unpleasant might happen."

"Yes, sir."

"Charlie," his father said, jabbing the air again like a boxer, "everything in life is a risk. Is that going to keep you home?"

"No, sir."

Good-byes were made outside the doors of the church. Alice—and a bunch of girls—were being picked up by her mother. They were all going to sleep at Alice's house. The car was so full of giggling girls there was no room for Charlie to be driven home.

"No problem," he said. "I can walk." With a bouncy wave he started off.

St. Anne's was located on Montague Street. Even at that hour it was busy. There were restaurants, cafés, a bookstore, a food market, all of which stayed open late. Charlie, enjoying looking at people, feeling connected, walked lightheartedly. He felt pleased about himself, glad he had gone to the dance. Alice had even paid attention to him. In the back of his mind he could almost hear his father asking him, "How was the dance?" Charlie would be able to say, "Cool." Moreover he would say it casually, as if that was all that needed to be said. They would touch fists and grin. Biderbiks don't cry.

From Montague Street Charlie turned onto Willow Street, his own street. It was a narrow street of old brownstone houses, none of which were more than a few stories high. Many had been converted into apartments. Old-fashioned street lamps—prickly with wrought-iron curlicues—shed weak, pinkish light. Tightly parked cars, dark and lumpish, seemed abandoned. A few spindly pin oak trees—leaves brittle and brown—cast lacelike shadows on the pavement made of cracked slate. As Charlie walked he could hear his own footsteps. After the raucous music of the dance, it was eerily quiet.

Just as Charlie began to grow aware that he was the only one on the street, he heard a whistle. The whistle was low but distinct—like the call of a night bird. It seemed to come from behind him.

Charlie paid no mind to it, but when he heard another whistle—in front of him—he stopped and tried to see where it came from. It was too dark.

Was someone after him? His heart began to race. He made a quick calculation. He was four blocks from his house. Though he told himself to run, he didn't. He was too unsure of himself. Instead, he listened intently.

Another whistle came. As before it came from behind him, but it was closer. Looking quickly over his shoulder, Charlie began to walk faster.

When another whistle came from in front of him he halted. Then a whistle came from the right side of the street. Charlie peered into the darkness. That time he thought he saw someone lurking behind a car.

Once more he told himself to run, but didn't. He was incapable of thinking and doing. He was in the grip of fear.

Now whistles came simultaneously from three sides. Charlie looked first in one direction, then another. Boys were drawing closer. How many there were he could not tell. They were darting forward, stopping, keeping to the shadows, surrounding him.

Charlie found it hard to breathe. His heart was hammering painfully. He kept telling himself to run. But it was too late.

"Hey, kid," a voice called.

Charlie spun toward the direction from which the call came. A tall, gangly teenager stepped out from behind a car. He wore a black jacket salted with silver studs. The sleeves were too short for his arms. His dangling hands, long and thin, were very white. He was too far away for Charlie to see his face.

Charlie turned in another direction. More boys stepped out of the shadows. No matter which way Charlie looked he saw them. His stomach knotted with tension. He was panting for breath.

The boys walked slowly, sauntering casually toward him. Gradually—by the pink light of the street lamps—their faces became distinct. Charlie knew none of them, though he thought he recognized one or two from the dance. Some were tall. A few were short and appeared quite young. Some had long sideburns and wispy goatees. Two had burning cigarettes in their mouths. All of them formed a circle about Charlie and stood there, staring at him silently.

Realizing he was trapped, an overwhelming sense of dread filled Charlie. In all his fourteen years he had never been so frightened.

"Enjoy the dance, kid?" one of the boys said.

Charlie peered around to see who had spoken.

"Over here, kid. Me."

He was not the tallest of the boys. His face was plump, his eyes large. An unlit cigarette dangled from his lips. He looked like every TV bad guy Charlie had ever seen.

"Hey, kid," the boy said, "I asked you if you enjoyed the dance."

"Wh . . . what?" Charlie stammered. He was struggling for breath so much he found it difficult to speak.

"The kid's a retard," someone said. Others laughed at the joke.

"I'm going to say it one last time: You have a good time at the dance?"

"Yes," Charlie managed to say, struggling to keep from bursting into tears.

"Got any money on you?"

Charlie reached a shaking hand into a pocket. He took out a dollar bill and a few coins.

"That's all," he said.

Someone stepped forward and snatched the money away. Two coins fell to the pavement. Charlie automatically moved toward them.

"Leave 'em!" the boy snapped. "They ain't yours anymore. Charlie pulled back.

"Now look here kid—what's your name . . . ?"

"Ch-Charlie. . . ."

"Charlie Boy. That's cool. You want to get out of this circle, Charlie Boy, you have to fight one of us."

Charlie wasn't sure he had heard right. "What?" he said. It was as if he were drowning in cement.

"I said you're going to have to fight one of us."

Fight. Charlie's stomach clenched. His father's words— "What's important is how you put up a fight"—flashed through his mind. He tried to lift his arms and make fists. His fingers would not work. He was too frightened. All he could say was, "Why?"

"The kid asks why."

The other boys laughed.

"Because I said so, that's why. When you go to St. Anne's you have to pay your dues. Fighting is your dues."

"I . . . I don't want to fight."

"Hey, Charlie, you got no choice. Go on. Look around. Pick whoever you want. Take the smallest. Don't matter. Hey, Pinky, you're the smallest. You do it."

One of the boys—smaller than the rest—moved out of the circle toward Charlie. His hands were up. He was grinning.

Charlie shook his head. "I don't want to fight," he said and began to back up.

The smaller boy kept advancing by prancing on his toes, waving his hands, smirking.

Charlie, backing up, bumped into the circle. Hands shoved him back toward the center. The small boy darted forward and struck Charlie in the face.

Without thinking, Charlie put up one arm to protect himself, even as he swung out wildly with his other arm.

Suddenly, he felt a blow on his head. Exploding light filled his eyes. His knees buckled, and he fell heavily to the ground. For a moment he lost consciousness. When he opened his eyes he saw feet all around him.

He heard, ". . . you hit him too hard, idiot! You could have killed him."

Charlie kept still. Even when he felt a sharp kick on his leg, he remained motionless. He could hear himself thinking: *Stay still! If they think they've hurt me maybe they'll go away.*

Sure enough someone said, "Hey, I think he must be hurt really bad."

"Beat it!" came the cry. Charlie heard the sound of running feet. Then silence.

Still on the pavement, Charlie waited. Cautiously he peeked up, wanting to make sure no one was there. He saw no one. Slowly, he lifted his head and looked around. The boys had gone.

He pushed himself to his feet. There was some dizziness. His head and leg were sore. Limping, whimpering, he began to run for home.

When he reached his front door, he was too shaky to use his key. Instead he pushed the doorbell. It was his mother—in her bathrobe—who opened the door. Charlie almost fell into the house.

In the living room his father was sitting in his easy chair, newspaper in hand.

Trying to keep from bursting into tears, Charlie, almost choking, cried, "I got beat up," and collapsed onto the couch.

Mrs. Biderbik, arms extended, started to move toward her son. Instead, stifling a cry, she rushed to the bathroom and returned with a damp cloth.

Mr. Biderbik leaned over his son. "You all right?" he asked.

Charlie nodded. As his mother wiped the dirt away from his face and forehead, a feeling of enormous relief filled him.

"What happened?" his father asked.

Haltingly, beneath the intent eyes of his father and mother, Charlie told his story.

When he was done, his mother, hovering between tears and fury, said, "I'm going to call the police."

Rather curtly, Mr. Biderbik said, "Don't waste your time. It's too late for them to do anything."

Nonetheless Mrs. Biderbik reached for the phone.

"Molly!" Mr. Biderbik barked, "leave it!"

"People should know," she objected, but didn't touch the phone.

Charlie's father pulled up a chair so he could be close to his son. "Now," he said, "how many did you say there were?"

Charlie, covering his face with his hands, sniffed. "I'm not sure. Maybe fifteen."

"Fifteen. And how many did they say you had to fight?"

There was something in Mr. Biderbik's voice that made Charlie look up. "Ah . . . one."

"One," repeated Mr. Biderbik slowly. "And what did you do?"

Charlie stared into his father's gray eyes. They seemed to be burning into him. "I, you know, kept asking them why I had to fight," he said.

"You've already said that," his father said, irritation in his voice. "I asked you what *you* did."

Charlie began to feel defensive. "I . . . told you. Nothing. I was too scared."

"Too scared," Mr. Biderbik echoed.

Charlie was sure he was sneering at him. "Then they hit me," he explained, "from behind. I think it was with a stick." He put his hand to his head. He could feel a lump. "And when I lay there, I think they must have thought they had killed me or something. So I just stayed there."

"You just *stayed* there?" Mr. Biderbik asked.

Charlie sniffed. "Yeah. So they would leave me alone." With a sickening feeling he turned away from his father's unfriendly eyes.

Mrs. Biderbik intervened. "Ted, I think it would be a good idea if Charlie got some sleep. We can deal with this in the morning. Sweetheart," she said to Charlie, "do you want a snack before bed?"

Charlie realized he was hungry. "A sandwich would be great." He moved to get up.

Mr. Biderbik held out a large hand, preventing Charlie from moving. "Wait a minute. Hold on. I need to make sure I understood. You just lay there. Is that correct? *Pretending* you were hurt."

Charlie, sensing his father's contempt, could feel nothing but shame. "Yeah," he murmured.

"Why?"

"Because . . . if I got up they would have . . . knocked me down again. Hurt me."

"Charlie . . . you could have . . . put up some . . . resistance. Don't you think?"

Charlie whispered, "Dad . . . there were a lot of them."

"You told me they said you only had to fight *one.*"

Mrs. Biderbik hurried up with a sandwich on a plate as well as a glass of milk. "Ted, leave the boy alone, for God's sake! He's been hurt. He's upset. You're not in court."

Mr. Biderbik, backing away, picked up his newspaper. First he rolled it up, then used it to slap the palm of his open hand twice. Frowning, he took one more look at his son, then stalked out of the room.

Though he knew the answer, Charlie whispered, "What's bugging him?"

"He's upset, that's all."

Charlie looked at the doorway. "He's disappointed with me. For not fighting." He struggled to resist tears.

"Charlie, love, don't be silly. Your father loves you a lot. Just eat a little something." She stroked his brow. "I'm glad you're okay. What a terrible thing. . . . Were you very frightened?"

"Yeah," Charlie replied, pulling away from his mother, and biting into the sandwich. As he ate he kept watching the doorway in hopes his father would come back. But he feared it too.

Next morning when Charlie woke he had a headache. Reaching up, he felt a sore spot at the back of his head. Though it felt tender the lump was down.

He lay quietly. How good it was to be in bed, safe. Eyes closed, he thought through what had happened. He didn't care what his father said. He was glad he hadn't fought. They might have killed him. It was done and gone.

Rolling over, he looked at the clock. It was almost nine. Quickly, he showered, pulled on jeans and a T-shirt, then went barefooted to the kitchen.

Dirty dishes were in the sink. The morning newspaper lay on the counter. It had been read. The house seemed deserted.

Charlie was looking for a note from his parents telling him where they were when the telephone rang. He picked it up.

" 'Lo."

"Hi. This is Mary Jane." Mary Jane was his mother's best friend. "Is this Charlie?"

"Yup."

"Oh, Charlie, your mother told me what happened last night. I'm *so* sorry. Are you all right?"

"Yeah, sure. Fine."

"Thank goodness! You read about these things, and then it happens to someone you care about. Makes me so angry. I'm so relieved you're feeling okay."

"Did you want to speak to my mom?" Charlie asked.

"If she's there. Charlie, I'm so glad you're all right."

Charlie went to the kitchen door and bellowed out, "Ma! Telephone!"

When there was no answer he returned to the phone. "Mary Jane, I don't think she's here. I don't know where she is. I'll tell her you called."

"Thank you, Charlie. Do take care of yourself."

Charlie made himself a breakfast of bacon and eggs, then sorted the newspaper and found the sports section and looked to see what football games would be on that weekend. He and his dad usually watched at least one game together.

The phone rang again.

" 'Lo."

"Charlie! Hey, how are you, buddy? This is Uncle Tim. Your mom told me what happened. You doing okay?"

"Yeah, sure."

"Good for you. Hey, don't let it get you down. I'm telling you, cities. You should move up here. Nothing like that here."

"I might."

"You do that."

"Want me to tell Ma you called?"

"No, no. I already spoke to her. It was you I wanted to talk to."

Before he had finished his breakfast he heard from two more of his mother's friends. Both inquired about him, what had happened, if he was all right. The calls made him feel good. People cared about him.

Then Arlo called. "How was the dance?"

Charlie told him about what happened both during the dance and after.

"I warned you stuff like that happens there, man," Arlo said sympathetically. "You couldn't drag me to one of those dances. I like living too much."

The two boys talked and made plans to meet later in the day. Just as Charlie was finishing up, his parents returned. They had been doing the weekly shopping at the supermarket.

"Morning, sweetheart," his mother called. "How you feeling?"

"Fine." As he helped unload the paper bags, Charlie kept glancing at his father. Mr. Biderbik had remained silent. His look was glum.

"Does your head hurt?" Charlie's mother asked.

"Not really," he said. "There were a bunch of calls."

His mother looked around.

Charlie listed the callers.

"What did they want?"

"They were . . . asking about me. I guess you told them about last night."

"People need to know."

"Yeah," said Charlie, stealing an imploring glance at his father, "but how come they're all calling?"

Mr. Biderbik looked around sharply. His face was ashen, his eyes cold. "They want to know how you got out of a fight," he said and marched out of the kitchen.

Charlie, stunned, stared after him.

His mother came up to him. Touched his arm. "Oh, Charlie, he didn't mean that. He's just—"

Charlie shrugged her off. He felt tears building. "He thinks I'm a coward, doesn't he?"

"Oh, love, of course he doesn't. He's just very concerned about the whole thing. Thinks we have to do something."

"What?"

"I don't know."

Charlie bolted from the kitchen, went to his room, slammed the door, and threw himself on his unmade bed. Hands under his head, staring at the ceiling, he replayed what had happened the night before. And he remembered what his father had said, "Biderbiks don't cry."

"I'm not a coward," he told himself. "I'm not. They would have killed me."

He would not let himself cry.

The following Tuesday evening, during dinner, Mr. Biderbik announced he had arranged a meeting that would be held on the following Thursday at St. Anne's Church. "I'm going to do something about this gang problem," he informed his wife and son.

Charlie felt as if he had been slapped across the face.

"I'd like you to call as many families as you know," his father instructed Mrs. Biderbik. "Tell them about the meeting. I intend to use this incident to organize parents. They should bring their teenage children. We have to make sure such things like this don't happen again."

"Things like what?" Charlie asked. He was certain his father was really referring to his not fighting.

His father gave him a cold glance, but didn't reply. Instead he said, "Dr. Mellon, the church rector, has agreed to cooperate. He doesn't have much choice. I told him the church had some responsibility for what happened. These dances have to have better security. One of the things he agreed to do is hold boxing lesson for boys. Apparently there's a small gym in the church rectory basement. Perfect place."

"Boxing lessons?" Charlie said incredulously.

Mr. Biderbik nodded. "Right. Twice a week. Seven-thirty. Till nine. You start next week. I've arranged for a good young teacher."

"But . . . I don't want to."

"Why?"

"I hate fighting."

"Charlie, my boy, you don't have a choice."

"Don't you care how I feel about a meeting?"

"Frankly, no. Charlie, the meeting is going to happen and you're going to be there—like it or not."

Charlie bolted from the table and lay upon his bed. Once again he thought of what had happened that night. How his father had reacted. How he himself felt. He thought about the calls that had come. They hadn't criticized him. But over and over again he heard his father's words, "They want to know how you got out of a fight."

"I'm not a coward," Charlie said out loud. "I'm not." He began to feel an anger toward his father such as he had never felt before. He clenched and unclenched his hands. He felt like hitting him. Hard.

The meeting was held in the rectory building adjacent to St. Anne's. It was a long, rectangular meeting room with dark wood paneling on the walls. A glittering chandelier hung from the ceiling. Twenty parents were in attendance, along with many of their children. They sat in folding chairs.

When Charlie came into the room with his father and mother he was extremely tense. Quickly, he glanced around to see who was there. To his horror he saw a few kids he knew. They were staring at him. As were others. In haste Charlie averted his eyes and stared at the floor.

Mr. Biderbik went to the front of the room. Charlie stayed with his mother and sat in the front row. Certain the whole room was staring at him, he could almost feel the eyes staring at his back. He entwined his fingers tightly. Now and again he glanced up at his father with angry eyes.

A heavy oak table had been placed at the front of the room. A pitcher of ice water and two glasses sat on it. Sitting next to Mr. Biderbik was Dr. Mellon, the rector. A short, slim, gray-haired man with bushy eyebrows, he kept his hands clasped.

The meeting had been called for seven-thirty. At twenty before the hour, Dr. Mellon whispered a few words to Mr. Biderbik, then stood up.

"Good evening," the rector began. His hands were folded and his voice sounded mellow. "And may God's Grace be on you all. My name is Dr. Mellon, and I should like to welcome you all to St. Anne's. I do regret that it took an unfortunate incident to bring you here."

Charlie felt himself blush.

"However," continued the rector, "at St. Anne's, we have a great desire to be part of the neighborhood. Anything that we can do to contribute to the neighborhood's well-being shall have our wholehearted support and blessings. Now, I should like to call upon Mr. Biderbik—who was kind enough to organize this gathering—to speak."

Mr. Biderbik came to his feet. He looked around before speaking. Then he said, "Good evening. My name is Ted Biderbik, a parent. I have a home on Willow Street. That's my wife and son in the front row.

"I want to thank Dr. Mellon for welcoming us here. And you all for coming.

"This meeting has been called to protect our children. Last Friday evening, following the dance held at the church, there was an unfortunate incident in which my son was set upon by a gang. He had been at the dance, and when walking home, some fifteen, twenty young men assaulted him. Though my boy put up a stiff resistance, there were too many of them to—"

During his father's remarks, Charlie, his heart beating wildly, had not even looked up. Now, abruptly he stood. All faces turned toward him.

Mr. Biderbik, looking puzzled, said, "Charlie, I am talking."

"That's not what happened," Charlie said. It was a struggle to get the words out.

"Charlie," Mr. Biderbik barked, "sit down!"

Mrs. Biderbik pulled at her son. "Charlie," she whispered. He stepped away.

"What happened," he continued, his voice growing stronger, his eyes squarely on his father, "is that these . . . guys surrounded me. . . ."

"Charlie!" cried his father.

"And told me I had to fight one of them. Any one. Even the smallest. But I was too scared to. See, I was . . . very frightened. . . . So I just lay there . . . hoping they would go away. And they did. Then I ran home."

The room became absolutely still.

Charlie swallowed hard and spoke again. "But . . . but my father . . . he thinks I was a coward. He thinks I should have . . . fought. It doesn't . . . matter to him that I could . . . have been hurt. Or killed. That's why my father called this meeting. It's not to protect the neighborhood. It's because my father is ashamed of his son. This meeting is for him. He's afraid that people will think badly of him. Because of me. But I think . . . he's the coward."

Mr. Biderbik, face red with embarrassment, stood before the table, staring at his son. He opened his mouth but no words came out.

Charlie, watching the pain gather on his father's face, suddenly felt overwhelmed with grief. It was then that he started to cry. For his father's sake.

About the Authors

AVI is the author of more than twenty-five books for young adults, including *Nothing But the Truth* and *The True Confessions of Charlotte Doyle,* both Newbery Honor books. *The Barn* was an ALA Notable Book and *Booklist* Editors' Choice selection, and *The Fighting Ground* was a winner of the Scott O'Dell Award. His other books include *The Man Who Was Poe, A Place Called Ugly, Who Stole the Wizard of Oz?, Romeo and Juliet Together (and Alive!) at Last, Blue Heron,* and *Sometimes I Think I Hear My Name.*

JOAN BAUER is the author of *Squashed,* a winner of the Delacorte Press Prize for First Young Adult Novel and a *School Library Journal* Best Book of 1992. Her other books include *Thwonk,* an ALA Best Book for Young Adults, and *Sticks,* a Junior Library Guild selection.

JAY BENNETT is a two-time winner of the Edgar Award. He has written more than a dozen books for young adults, including *The Long Black Coat, The Dangling Witness, The Executioner, I Never Said I Loved You, The Skeleton Man,* and *Sing Me a Death Song.* He has also written extensively for both radio and television.

JUDITH GOROG is the author of *In a Creepy, Creepy Place and Other Scary Stories* and *In a Messy Room and Other Scary Stories.* Her other books include *When Nobody's Home* and *Ol' Bones and Other Grave Delights.*

HERB KARL is a teacher first and a writer second. His first young adult novel was *The Toom County Mud Race,* an honorable mention for the Delacorte Press Prize for First Young Adult Novel, and an ALA Recommended Books for Reluctant Young Readers selection. *Mud Race* was written originally as a screenplay and was a winner of the Florida Governor's Screenwriting Competition. Karl has written several other screenplays and stories and is at work on a new young adult novel.

GORDON KORMAN has written more than ten books for young adults, including three ALA Best Books for Young Adults winners, *Son of Interflux, A Semester in the Life of a Garbage Bag,* and *Losing Joe's Place. The Twinkie Squad* was a Junior Library Guild selection, *No Coins, Please* won the Air Canada Award, and *Why Did the Underwear Cross the Road* was a Book-of-the-Month Club selection.

WALTER DEAN MYERS is the author of *Somewhere in the Darkness* and *Scorpions,* both Newbery Honor Books. In addition, he has won the Coretta Scott King Award five times. An author of more than thirteen books for young adults, Myers has won the Boston Globe/Horn Book Award, twice the ALA Best Books for Young Adults Award, the Margaret A. Edwards Award, the ALAN Award, the Parents' Choice Award, and twice the Golden Kite Honor Book Award.

JOAN LOWERY NIXON is a record nine-time nominee and the only four-time winner of the Edgar Award for Best Juvenile Mystery for *The Kidnapping of Christina Lattimore, The Seance, The Other Side of Dark,* and *The Name of the Game Was Murder.* She is a winner of the Spur Award from the Western Writers Association, the California's Young Reader's Medal (twice), Indiana's Young Hoosier Book Award (three times), and Nevada's Young Reader's Award (twice).

RICHARD PECK is a two-time winner of the Edgar Award and the author of more than ten books for young adults, including *Ghosts I Have Been, The Ghost Belonged to Me, Don't Look and It Won't Hurt,* and *Are You in the House Alone?*

He is the recipient of the Margaret A. Edwards Award and winner of the National Council of Teachers of English/ALAN Award. He won the 1991 Medallion from the University of Southern Mississippi and *The Last Safe Place on Earth* was named an ALA Best Book for Young Adults.

SUSAN BETH PFEFFER is the author of more than fifty books for children and young adults. *Kid Power* was the winner of the Dorothy Canfield Fisher Award and the Sequoyah Children's Book Award. *About David* won the South Carolina Young Adult Book Award, and *The Year Without Michael* again won the South Carolina Young Adult Book Award and was named a Best 100 Books for Teenagers from 1967–1993 by the American Library Association. Her most recent books include *Twice Taken, Family of Strangers, Nobody's Daughter,* and *Justice for Emily.*

NEAL SHUSTERMAN is the author of many award-winning novels, including *Scorpion Shards,* a New York Public Library Books for the Teen Age selection, and *The Eyes of Kid Midas,* an ALA Best Book for the Reluctant Young Reader Award winner. *What Daddy Did* was an ALA Best Books for Young Adults Award winner and an International Reading Association Young Adult Choice Award winner. His other books include *Speeding Bullet,* nominated for the California Young Reader Medal, *Dissidents, The Shadow Club, The Dark Side of Nowhere,* and the short story collections, *Mindquakes, Mindstorms,* and *Mindtwisters.*

NANCY SPRINGER twice won the Edgar Award for *Looking for Jamie Bridger* and *Toughing It.* In addition, *Toughing It* was a Carolyn W. Field Award Honor Book, an ALA Best Books for Young Adults Award winner, and an ALA Recommended Books for Reluctant Young Readers selection. Her book *Colt* was an IRA Young Adults Choice Award winner and a Joan Fassler Memorial Book Award winner.

SUZANNE FISHER STAPLES is the author of *Shabanu,* a Newbery Honor Book and an ALA Notable Children's Book Award winner, an ALA Best Books for Young Adults and an IRA Young Adults' Choice Award winner. It also won the Joan Sugerman Award for Excellence in Literature and was chosen a *New York Times* Best Books for Young Adults. *Haveli* won a Parents' Choice Award and was an ALA Notable Book selection. Her most recent novel, *Dangerous Skies,* was on the *Publishers Weekly* Best Books for 1996 list and was a New York Public Library "Best Hundred Books" selection.

VIRGINIA EUWER WOLFF is the author of *Make Lemonade,* an ALA Best Books for Young Adults and an ALA Recommended Books for Reluctant Readers Award winner, a Golden Kite Award and the Oregon Book Award winner, a *School Library Journal* Best Book, and was chosen as a *Booklist* Top of the List and a Parents Choice Award winner. *Probably Still Nick Swanson* won the IRA Children's Choice Award, the ALA Best Book for Young Adult Award, and was a *School Library Journal* Best Book. In addition she is the author of *The Mozart Season,* an ALA Notable Book for Children and an ALA Best Books for Young Adults Award winner.

SHARON DENNIS WYETH is the author of eight books for young people, including *Always My Dad,* which was selected by the New York Public Library as one of the Best 100 Books of 1995. In addition, it was a "Reading Rainbow" selection. Her other books include *The World of Daughter McGuire, Vampirebugs, Boys Wanted, Boy Crazy,* and *Ginger Brown: Too Many Houses.*